# Callie stood only a few feet away from Joel.

She was so close he could almost reach out and touch her, but he controlled his desire.

"They have a sense about them, horses do. It was a tough day, Joel, and I'm sure they're glad to be home."

"We all are. Thank you for keeping yourself and my girl safe this afternoon. I'll be forever grateful."

Callie smiled and he wanted to drop to his knees right there. A mere thank-you didn't seem like enough. Not only was he grateful for his daughter's safety, but he now realized just how grateful he was for Callie's safety. He couldn't handle it if anything happened to either one of them.

"Not a problem. I was only doing what I'd been trained to do from years of driving a truck on my ranch."

He took a step closer, hoping she wouldn't move away. He felt drawn to her, as if he'd lost all power over his emotions.

Dear Reader,

I love writing about the characters that inhabit the small town of Briggs, Idaho. They never cease to amaze me, especially the children.

Each time I sit down to write a new book, I think I know my characters inside and out, but somewhere during the course of writing their story they take on their own identities. Suddenly, the past I carefully designed for each character doesn't meet their needs, so they up and change it. What's even more surprising is when they change a secret desire I clearly thought they needed. Most of the time, it turns out to be something completely different than what I'd planned.

That's the writing process...at least for me.

This story took on a darker tone than most of my books, with a deeper meaning. I wanted to delve into betrayal and loss, but I never expected to also take on abandonment, forgiveness and, eventually, acceptance.

That's not to say all the humor is gone. It's not. But this time, it's wrapped in a bit more drama than I had originally intended.

I hope you enjoy *A Cowboy in Her Arms* as much as I enjoyed writing it.

Please come visit me on Twitter, @maryleoauthor, or at Facebook.com/maryleoauthor, and while you're there, please sign up for my newsletter.

All my best,

*Mary*

# A COWBOY
# IN HER ARMS

—

### MARY LEO

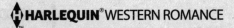

HARLEQUIN® WESTERN ROMANCE

Recycling programs
for this product may
not exist in your area.

ISBN-13: 978-0-373-75748-0

A Cowboy in Her Arms

Copyright © 2017 by Mary Leo

All rights reserved. Except for use in any review, the reproduction or
utilization of this work in whole or in part in any form by any electronic,
mechanical or other means, now known or hereinafter invented, including
xerography, photocopying and recording, or in any information storage
or retrieval system, is forbidden without the written permission of the
publisher, Harlequin Enterprises Limited, 225 Duncan Mill Road,
Don Mills, Ontario M3B 3K9, Canada.

This is a work of fiction. Names, characters, places and incidents are
either the product of the author's imagination or are used fictitiously,
and any resemblance to actual persons, living or dead, business
establishments, events or locales is entirely coincidental.

This edition published by arrangement with Harlequin Books S.A.

For questions and comments about the quality of this book,
please contact us at CustomerService@Harlequin.com.

® and TM are trademarks of Harlequin Enterprises Limited or its
corporate affiliates. Trademarks indicated with ® are registered in the
United States Patent and Trademark Office, the Canadian Intellectual
Property Office and in other countries.

Printed in U.S.A.

*USA TODAY* bestselling author **Mary Leo** grew up in South Chicago in the tangle of a big Italian family. She's worked in Hollywood, Las Vegas and Silicon Valley. Currently she lives in San Diego with her husband, author Terry Watkins, and their sweet kitty, Sophie. Visit her website at maryleo.com.

### Books by Mary Leo

### Harlequin American Romance

*Falling for the Cowboy*
*Aiming for the Cowboy*
*Christmas with the Rancher*
*Her Favorite Cowboy*
*A Christmas Wedding for the Cowboy*

Visit the Author Profile page
at Harlequin.com for more titles.

For Kathryn Lye, who has always believed
in my work, and championed each of my books.
You're simply the best!

# Prologue

Joel Darwood tried to take in what Mrs. Bradshaw was saying about his daughter, Emma, being disruptive to the class, causing the teacher to have to reprimand her after she bonked Jimmy Slater in the head with her baguette during lunch. He knew exactly where this conversation was heading. This was the third preschool his daughter would be expelled from, and she wasn't even five years old yet. What would happen when she was in regular school?

"Fortunately, no one was hurt during the attack," Mrs. Bradshaw said, looking as though the baguette could have caused immeasurable damage.

"It was a baguette, still fresh from this morning when I picked it up at the bakery down the street. I hardly think we could consider it a weapon."

"Maybe so, but she struck him."

"Jimmy is a full two inches taller than Emma, and if I have the story right, he swiped her Juicy Juice box and was taunting her with it."

Mrs. Bradshaw grinned, seeming self-righteous as she intertwined her fingers, then rested her hands on the desk in front of her. "That's hardly a reason to smack him with her lunch. Plus, as you know, this isn't the first time Emma has disrupted the class. There were two other incidents that were far worse."

"I wouldn't call asking for seconds on orange slices or refusing to go outside for recess when it was windy and snowing disrupting the class."

"It might not have been so bad if she had simply told her teacher she didn't want to go outside, but she inspired the entire class to rebel. Her behavior is quite unacceptable. Emma needs to learn how to follow rules, and so far, your child demonstrates signs of becoming a rabble-rouser, something we cannot abide here at Mission Academy. Therefore, I'm afraid, Emma is no longer welcome at the academy."

"So you're expelling her?"

"Yes, I'm afraid so."

"No need to be afraid. We'll leave peacefully. I already ate my baguette on the way over."

"Excuse me?"

Joel stood as a grin tightened his lips. "There is no excuse for you or this restrictive school. Good day, Mrs. Bradshaw. Oh, and by the way, I'd rather my daughter be a *rabble-rouser* than a complacent doormat. And if that's what it takes to be part of Mission Academy, you can take your school and…"

But he didn't finish the statement. Instead, he widened his grin, spun on his heels and marched out of the room, careful not to slam the door behind him.

As he walked to his SUV, all he could think of was how he and his daughter needed a change…a big change. One of those start-over kinds of changes that inspired new beginnings in new surroundings. Heck, he needed it as much as his daughter. Neither of them had any reason to remain in Boise, especially now when Joel's position at his dad's accounting firm seemed to be going nowhere fast.

Unlike his dad, Joel had never been all that interested in crunching numbers. He only majored in accounting in college because his dad had expected him to. Joel had found his job incredibly tedious and would try to avoid doing anything too complicated by handing off some of their best clients to one of his contemporaries. Joel was more of an embarrassment rather than the prodigal son who would one day inherit the business.

A change of venue might be exactly what the doctor ordered.

# Chapter One

The cream-colored stallion whinnied and stomped his heavy hoof, eager to get this show on the road. It took all of Callie Grant's riding skills to keep Apple Sammy from taking off before it was time to begin the parade, which stretched out for at least three blocks behind them, including all the side streets.

Lawn chairs had been set out along the route as placeholders for the townsfolk the night before. Every child under the age of ten had an undisputed spot at the front of the sidewalk, joined by seniors over the age of eighty, especially the town's elderly military heroes. Anyone who had served in the military was considered a hero in this small town nestled in the Teton Valley, and was treated as such. No one spoke of these rules. They were simply woven into the tapestry of everyday life here in Briggs, Idaho, home of the mighty russet potato.

Now that the parade participants were lined up and eager to go, the sounds of their excited chatter echoed off of each shop and residence along Main Street. The teens in the marching band, dressed in gold, red and white, the official school colors from Ronald Reagan High School, readied themselves directly behind Callie. They seemed about as anxious as Apple Sammy. Fortunately, their director, Mr. Harwood, head of the music program at the school, knew how to corral his fifty or so students much better than Callie was able to control one determined horse.

Apple Sammy pulled back and whinnied once again as Mr. Harwood gave the direction for the band to begin its first tune, "The Star-Spangled Banner," which just about blew out Callie's eardrums. Sadly, she'd forgotten her earplugs.

It was Western Days in Briggs, Idaho, which meant the only Miss Russet, Callaghan—Callie—Grant, who had won the coveted title for her hometown, took the center spot between the Misses, directly in front of the marching band in this year's parade. Not that Callie wanted the hallowed position, nor did she still particularly enjoy the title. The Miss Russet sparkly tiara had long lost its appeal and riding in the annual parade dressed in her best cowgirl wear no longer generated any excitement.

After ten years of participating in countless parades and community events, she would gladly hand over the reins to any other Miss Russet her fair town could produce. Unfortunately, no other contestant from Briggs had won the coveted title since that fortuitous day.

Callie hadn't even entered the pageant the year she'd won. Her sneaky sister Coco was responsible for that effort, and once the die was cast, Callie had no choice but to go along with the program. Her family was much too delighted at the prospect of a win for her to back out. Could she help it if her biggest competition that year was Helga Schnook, whose yodel sounded more like nails on a chalkboard than an actual yodel? Callie had tried to downplay her own talent, playing the piano, by picking "The Minute Waltz" by Chopin, thinking it was a relatively short and uncomplicated piece compared to some of the others she'd played in previous recitals and competitions. Unfortunately, that year, Helga and the other contenders had woefully failed to deliver any real talent, so the judges had unanimously chosen Callaghan Grant, from Briggs, Idaho, as Miss Russet, solidifying her now long-standing title…a title she now wished she had never won.

The biggest reason for her disenchantment for participating in the parade this year happened to be her age. At twenty-eight and twenty pounds heavier than when she picked up her title, she felt awkward sandwiched in between paper-thin sixteen-year-old Jackie Winslow, the current Miss Russet who hailed from Firth, Idaho, and equally thin seventeen-year-old, Nellie Bent, Miss Briggs. Then there was the lovely and svelte Miss Idaho on the outer right flank, who hovered somewhere in her very early twenties, and the rough-and-tumble Miss Rodeo Queen, who didn't look a day over eighteen riding an obedient black stallion on the far left.

Callie had wanted to ride alongside the mayor and the president of the local Rotary Club, who were both much older than her, but the mayor wouldn't hear of it.

"Your place is with the reigning monarchy of Idaho," said Mayor Sally Hickman, a blond-haired, fortysomething beauty with a straight-talk, natural-born-leader disposition that had won her the last three terms, when Callie had approached her with the idea.

"But I haven't held the title in ten years! I shouldn't even be in the parade anymore. Who made up this rule, anyway? It really needs to change."

"You know very well the good people of Briggs expect to see you in the parade. You're the idol of every young girl in Briggs who hopes to grow up and follow in your footsteps one day. You certainly don't want to disappoint them, now do you?"

"Of course not, but—"

"Good, then, short of a personal catastrophe, I'll expect to see you in your usual place this year." And she dismissed Callie for her next appointment, which happened to be with Callie's older brother, Carson, who was grand marshal of this year's parade.

Carson had won the National Saddle Bronc Riding Championship in Las Vegas the previous December, and the town more or less worshipped him for it. Unlike Callie, Carson had no trouble accepting the town's accolades, which were well deserved.

Callie, on the other hand, wanted no part of it…at least not this year. She was starting her new position at Briggs Elementary in a few weeks, taking over as kindergarten teacher for Miss Sargent, who had retired last spring, and she wanted to be taken seriously. Not that winning the Miss Russet title wasn't a serious accomplishment, it was. But her pageant days were so far over that her tiara was beginning to rust.

Now her only hope was the current Miss Briggs, Nellie Bent, who needed a good solid talent in order to win the coveted title of Miss Russet. Sadly, suspicions on the street had it that Nellie couldn't hold a tune—at least no one had ever heard her sing— she couldn't play a serious musical instrument, nor could she dance. What had secured her title as Miss Briggs was her ability to jump rope, not exactly the kind of talent the Miss Russet judges were looking for, but then Callie hadn't seen the performance. Perhaps jumping rope took on a whole new cachet when Nellie did it.

Callie also knew Nellie had won a small scholarship to Idaho State, in Pocatello, a fine university if there ever was one, and Callie's alma mater. Surely Nellie wanted to add to that scholarship fund by winning Miss Russet, which came with a college scholarship of its own. Nellie could slip right into Callie's position in the Western Days parade and everyone would cheer her on, including Callie.

What young woman didn't want that?

According to Mayor Hickman, every young girl in Briggs did.

Just as Callie was about to ask Nellie about entering the contest, once the marching band took a breather, she spotted someone in the crowd that sent a chill up her spine. When she craned over Nellie, first leaning forward in the saddle, then back to get a better look, that person had vanished into the crowd.

Or was never there in the first place.

"Is everything okay?" Nellie asked as she waved and smiled at the enthusiastic crowd who cheered and whistled as the Misses trotted by, their horses almost in sync with each other, heavy hooves click-clacking on the roadway. "You look a little pasty."

Callie settled in the saddle, grasping the horn as if her life depended on it. "I…I thought I saw someone I knew, but I must've been mistaken. He doesn't seem to be there now."

"An old boyfriend?"

Callie grinned at Nellie, amazed that she could be that insightful. "Yes, a very old boyfriend, from college. A boyfriend who I'd rather never see again."

Callie's heart still pounded against her chest at the thought of seeing Joel Darwood. She'd practiced what she would say to him if their paths ever crossed, but at the moment, all those well-crafted words seemed elusive. Her brain had turned into instant mush as soon as she thought she'd spotted him standing in the crowd.

"I have an ex-boyfriend like that," Nellie said. "He lives in Chubbuck now, and every time I see him I want to sock him in the gut. He cheated on me with a girl who can't even ride a horse or rope a steer."

Nellie couldn't have weighed more than a hundred pounds soaking wet, was no more than five foot two inches tall and seemed as delicate as a dandelion. "You can rope a steer?"

"I can do almost anything with a rope. I grew up with four older brothers."

Her jumping-rope abilities just bumped up a few notches. "Have you ever thought about entering the Miss Russet contest?"

"Actually, I—"

But Callie had stopped listening. She'd spotted that guy in the crowd again...that guy who looked exactly like Joel, only without his scruffy beard and long dark hair. This was the clean-cut version. Look-alike Joel's head had bobbed out between a group of people she didn't recognize. This false Joel had pulled a young child off his shoulders, and in doing so he'd looked down so Callie couldn't get a good look at his face, at his eyes. She'd know if it was really him once she could see his dreamy eyes. The real Joel Darwood had the kind of long dark eyelashes any girl would swoon over, and eyes so blue you'd swear they were part of the sky itself.

She jerked the reins a bit to slow Apple Sammy as she watched look-alike Joel take the child's hand, a girl from what she could make out, with features that looked familiar…too familiar.

As he made his way through the crowd, he glanced up, but not enough so she could get a clear shot of his face. He slipped a light gray cowboy hat on his head, tipped it forward on his forehead and he and the child made their way up the crowded sidewalk.

The Joel she knew would never wear a cowboy hat, so it couldn't possibly be him. The Joel she knew was more of the laid-back, chillin' type, rather than a working cowboy, and in these parts of Idaho, if a male of any age wore a cowboy hat, that meant he was a down-in-the-dirt, hardworking, hay-hauling, calf-roping, horse-breaking cowboy.

His walk…that swagger…no one had a sexy swagger like Joel Darwood and sure as the sun rose over the mountains every morning, this false Joel had that swagger.

"Hey, watch where you're going," a teen holding a tuba yelled as Callie sidestepped Apple Sammy.

Her horse had drifted back into the middle of the marching band without her being aware of the intrusion.

"Sorry… I'm sorry," Callie repeated over and over again as she tried to guide the ornery creature away from the group.

Unfortunately, getting Apple Sammy to mind her

wasn't exactly working, especially now that the band had started playing again. The loud music seemed to spook the poor creature and he didn't know which way to go to get away from it. His ears kept twitching as if the sound was so annoying he was trying to somehow muffle it by flattening his ears as best he could.

Now more band members yelled at her along with Mr. Harwood, their leader, who tried to grab on to the reins, which made Apple Sammy rear back, away from his touch.

"Get that horse out of here," Mr. Harwood yelled over the eardrum-piercing music.

Callie directed her horse to what she thought was out of the way of the band, when she nearly ran right into the Idaho potato float. The float veered away from her a little too quickly, causing the roly-poly potato people to literally bounce off the float and careen down the street with their hands and feet poking out of their costumes in a vain attempt to stop themselves from smacking into the crowds on the surrounding sidewalks.

"Save yourselves! Run for the hills," Callie yelled as the townsfolk scattered out of the way of the swirling potato people heading straight for them.

The band stopped playing.

The 4-H club float behind the potato float screeched to a halt. The kids holding on to the animals atop the float looked panic-stricken. The clowns stopped tossing candy into the crowd. Instead they stared in awe as the entire parade of decorated cars, trucks, tractors, another school band and an assortment of themed floats came to a grinding halt.

As the chaos ensued all around Callie, she watched

as cowboy Joel Darwood looked right at her with those smokin' blue eyes of his, gave a little shake of his head, turned and swaggered off behind the crowd, holding a little girl tightly in his arms.

JOEL KNEW HE'D have to run into Callaghan Grant at some point now that he was living in Briggs, but never in a million years did he think she might literally run him over with an entire parade. He hadn't expected her to have such an extreme reaction to his presence that she would cause a cataclysmic disaster in what was supposed to be a fun outing with his daughter and aunt.

Fortunately, no one was hurt, not even the people who were trapped inside the bouncy russet potato costumes.

Unfortunately, he was now officially scared to talk to Miss Russet Potato, aka Callaghan Grant. Okay, so maybe he wasn't scared exactly, but certainly apprehensive. He remembered that Callaghan had always been somewhat high-strung, deliriously determined and incredibly resourceful, but this kind of disruptive behavior was way over the top. There was no telling what she might do when they physically met…push him under a tractor perhaps?

From the alarmed look on her face, she just might be capable.

"Callie seems a little intense," Aunt Polly said once the parade had started up again. "Funny, but I don't remember her being that unruly as a child."

Joel had guided his daughter and aunt to a spot on the sidewalk completely hidden from Callaghan's view. Emma stood up front where Joel could keep an eye on her, but out of earshot from their conversation.

"It was always Sarah who got them into trouble, never Callie," Aunt Polly said. "She seemed cautious and reserved back then. Not that she wasn't feisty—she was—but mostly it was Sarah who led the way, and Callie would follow. Of course, that was a lot of years ago. I think Sarah stopped coming out for the summers when they were around thirteen. I remember how heartbroken Callie was when Sarah didn't show up that first summer."

"Maybe this was a mistake," Joel said, rethinking his need for a fresh start. Surrounding himself and his daughter with livestock and open spaces rather than city folk and tall buildings had never been his dream, but he knew he'd had to suck up his self-serving ego and become the father that Emma deserved. Problem was he'd moved to the one town in the entire country he and Sarah had avoided for good reason.

If anything he should have gone to a completely new town. Perhaps somewhere in Montana or Utah instead of Idaho, and more importantly, somewhere other than where Callaghan Grant lived.

"What? No. Kids love parades. Besides, no one was hurt. Emma's enjoying herself. I don't think she's traumatized over a few rolling human potatoes."

Polly had never been filled in on the details of Joel's connection to Callaghan Grant. His wife had made a conscious decision to not tell her, and Joel had no reason to try to change Sarah's mind. "I meant maybe this whole thing was a mistake…moving to Briggs with you."

Aunt Polly turned to face him just as another

marching band was passing by, the music loud and persistent. "Have you seen the look on your daughter's face?"

Emma turned at that moment, holding her ears but grinning despite any discomfort she might have had from the music.

"I know. I know. She seems to love it here," Joel told her, having to admit the obvious.

"It's exactly where she belongs right now. You, too. And me! I'm happier than a pig in mud to be home again, and you made that possible." She chuckled. "Ironic, but I used to hate living in this quirky little no-place town when my Daniel first moved me here from Boise. I thought I'd die of pitiful loneliness and boredom, but I didn't. I adjusted while Daniel was alive. Once I was on my own again, I headed straight back to the city thinking I'd love it. For a long time I did, loved everything about it. Until a real emptiness set in, the kind of emptiness that weighs on you like an early frost in autumn, making everything cold and brittle. The ranch, this town and the people in it had taken root in my soul. Too bad it took me almost twelve years of living in Boise again to realize that. Now that I'm back, ain't no way I'm ever leaving again."

"That's easy for you to say. You don't have Callaghan Grant to deal with."

"The Grants were always an ornery bunch, especially when they were kids, but like this town, they grow on you, and after a while, you can't shake either the Grants or anybody else in this town. They become part of who you are."

"If you say so."

Joel wasn't buying any of it. The mood he was in, he'd just as soon pack up right now and drive away… but watching Emma laughing and waving to the other kids in the parade, he knew staying put was the right thing to do.

Emma and her great-aunt had anticipated this parade for weeks and had even bought matching Western wear for the event, including Western hats. Emma had insisted on a pink one. Aunt Polly had drawn the line at a pink cowgirl hat, but otherwise the outfits were exactly the same: boot-cut jeans, blue checked shirts, wide leather belts with a shiny gold-colored buckle and brown boots. Ever since Emma had tried on her first pair of real cowgirl boots, she refused to wear anything else. Even when Aunt Polly managed to get a dress on her, she still wanted to wear her boots. If he didn't know better, he would think his daughter had picked up some of Callaghan's traits. Back in college, she rarely wore anything else on her feet. High heels or sneakers were the exception rather than the norm.

"I'm surprised she recognized you," Aunt Polly said.

Joel had gone through a metamorphosis of sorts in the last few months. Not only had he shaved off his beard, he'd cut his hair short and swapped his ratty-looking clothes for new jeans, Western shirts and a gray cowboy hat. He was working on changing his negative disposition, as well. Flight used to be his standard reaction to a problem or situation he didn't particularly want to deal with. Instead of handling the crisis, he'd leave the scene, hoping that by the time he returned—if he returned—the "crisis" would be resolved.

He could no longer afford that luxury.

He'd finally embraced the fact that he was a full-time single parent now, and his daughter depended on him not only for a decent roof over her head and food on the table, but for him to participate in her daily life. Instead of standing on the sidelines while one interchangeable babysitter after another raised her.

Deciding to move to Briggs had only been the beginning of his transformation. Now he had to learn what it meant to stick around, even when times got tough.

"The same can be said for Callaghan. She looked quite different in college. For one thing, her hair color was a lot lighter and she wore it shorter, sort of cropped tight against her neck."

Joel didn't want to mention how her body had changed, as well. She was a petite little thing in college, constantly worried about how many calories she ate on any given day. They'd had long discussions over her food intake, which wasn't much, while he'd tried to get her to eat a cheeseburger or drink a milk shake to get some meat on her bones. At one point he worried she might be suffering from anorexia.

Not anymore.

Callaghan now had the shapely body of a woman, a round and supple woman, instead of that wisp of a girl he'd known in college. Back then she prided herself on still being able to get into the same jeans she'd worn as a young teen.

Things had apparently changed.

Her raven-black hair now draped over her shoulders, cascading down her back in soft curls. He liked this new Callaghan Grant…maybe a little too much.

He knew he shouldn't be thinking such things, especially in light of all the pain he and his wife had caused her with their reckless behavior.

He had no room in his life for a relationship with any woman, and most assuredly not with Callaghan Grant, who undoubtedly still hated him.

"Oh, Daddy, look at all those bunnies and baby goats. I love baby goats, Daddy." Emma had turned slightly, grabbed Joel's hand and pulled him closer. The 4-H club float passed by and as it did, Emma clapped her hands and stood on her toes trying to get a better look.

"You do? I didn't know that," Joel said.

Then he swung her up onto his shoulders, giving her a clear view. Her little arms encircled his head, one hand patting his cheek. His heart always melted whenever Emma showed him any affection, almost as if it took him by surprise.

"I didn't know it either until just now. And baby pigs, too. And bunnies, I really love bunnies, Daddy."

He hadn't seen her get so excited about anything in months. He didn't want it to end, at least not yet. They followed the float as it made its way up the street in front of the local firefighters and military personnel, everyone waving and smiling. Fortunately, there was no sign of Callaghan anywhere. He wasn't in the mood for a confrontation. Not while his daughter seemed so interested in something other than the Elsa doll her mom had given her last summer.

When the float finally stopped, Joel immediately slipped her off his shoulders. They headed in closer to get a better look at the animals as some of the kids from the float along with a group of adults began off-loading them into cages from the back of a blue pickup truck.

"Can I pet one, Daddy? Can I?" Emma asked as Joel held on to her hand. Aunt Polly had stayed back, chatting with an old friend, Traci Sargent, a contemporary who seemed genuinely happy to see her. They had hugged and fussed over each other for at least five full minutes. From what Joel could make out, they'd been friends since Polly first arrived in Briggs…a fact that Joel missed in his life. His family had moved around Boise so much that he was never able to make long-lasting friends.

He hoped that wouldn't be the case for Emma.

Wade Porter, a rough-and-tumble cowboy in his early thirties was there, as well, fussing over Polly like he always did. Wade had leased Polly's grazing land for his horses and had kept an eye on things while renters were living in the ranch house and then during the years the house was empty. The *dude* seemed to attract women of all ages no matter where he went, and so far, Joel had no use for the guy and had taken an immediate disliking to him. Wade was too nice, too accommodating and much too helpful. Joel suspected there was some other motive running through him rather than pure friendliness…but so far, Joel couldn't make out what that other motive might be.

"If they'll let you, sure," Joel told Emma, giving her hand a reassuring squeeze.

Being this close to farm animals was new to Joel and his five-year-old daughter. He'd grown up in a city and had rarely wandered into the country. The closest he'd ever come to a farm animal was at the county fair when he'd walk through some of the tents, and even then, the calves, pigs and rabbit were either in a pen of some kind or locked inside a cage.

Besides, he never had an interest in those kinds of animals. He was more of a dog kind of guy, a husky or a retriever.

Emma, on the other hand, seemed to be all about baby goats and bunnies, especially the long-eared type of bunnies. There were two on the float—one was a deep orange color while the other was a dappled black-and-white. One ear of the dappled one was black along with one eye, and the rest of its body was mostly white with some speckled black. Joel had to admit, these little guys were possibly the cutest creatures he'd ever seen. Emma approached the boy holding the black-and-white bunny.

Other kids who had watched the parade had gathered around a white goat on a leash and a baby pig that tried its best to wiggle out of the arms of one of the young boys who was trying his best to hold on to the small creature.

"Oh, Daddy, she's so soft," Emma said as she cautiously ran her hand over the bunny's fat, round body. The boy, around ten or twelve, held the bunny as it rested in his arms, the bunny looking about as content as a kitten in the sun.

"His name is Wheezy. He's five months old and we've been training him to hop over hurdles," the boy told Emma. "He loves to jump, and he loves to be petted and played with."

"Do you play with him a lot?"

The boy nodded. "Whenever I can. He has four brothers and three sisters so sometimes it's hard to get to all of them."

"I don't have any bunnies. My daddy likes dogs, but I like bunnies."

"We have a dog, too, and chickens, and a lot of horses."

"We have horses, but I'd rather have a bunny." Emma couldn't seem to stop loving Wheezy, and as time passed she became more confident petting him. Until this moment, Joel hadn't considered that Emma might want a pet of her own. Yet another example of how woefully remiss he'd been in raising his daughter. The guilt would sometimes overwhelm him, but he'd learned how to pull himself back from the self-pity pit by making sure he was now 100 percent engaged in his current life…which was something he was still working on.

Emma glanced back at Joel, beaming, looking for his approval, which he gave with a hearty smile and nod.

Joel's heart swelled as he watched Emma ease in closer to the bunny, giving it long, gentle strokes. The boy holding the bunny kept chatting with Emma, asking her name and talking about the furry creature. Normally, his Emma barely spoke to other children, but for some reason, as she stroked the soft animal, she chatted up a storm. The boy, Buddy Granger, told Emma all about Wheezy, the medium-sized Holland lop, and the rest of the animals on his family's ranch, which was also some sort of riding school. Emma stood riveted to every word.

Ever since they had moved to the Double S Ranch, his daughter's entire demeanor had changed. Little by little, she was coming out of her shell, and the animals were helping. Aunt Polly had already brought in a couple horses, and two stray tabby cats had taken up residency inside the barn. Plus, he'd been thinking about adding a puppy to the mix soon, and now that he knew his daughter liked bunnies, he might consider building a bunny hutch to the vast array of projects that required his attention.

He knew living on a ranch was going to be a challenge, but he never dreamed it would be an endless string of physical work. Callaghan hadn't talked much about ranching or her Miss Russet title when they were dating…too tangled up with school activities, he supposed. Back then their days seemed to be consumed with class, homework, school activities and sex…lots of sex, until everything changed on the turn of a dime.

He cautiously looked around trying to spot Callaghan in the crowd, and so far the coast seemed clear. Although in a small town like this, he felt as though everyone already knew all about the sordid details of their breakup in college…and he was most certainly the bad guy in their version.

Which, to some extent, he was, but he refused to think about any of that now. At the moment, his total focus was centered on his daughter and her happiness. Every choice he made was entirely for her benefit, and if that included having to openly take the fall for what happened between him and Callaghan back in college so the citizens of Briggs would accept him and his daughter, then so be it.

He was out of options.

This was his last stop. He had to make it work no matter what he had to do to appease his ex. Briggs, Idaho, was her hometown. Her family and friends lived here, and despite everything that had happened, he would find a way to make peace with the girl he still cared about.

## Chapter Two

"That's him," Callie told her older sister Coco. The two women tried to hide behind a cluster of aspen trees. The parade had long since ended, the floats dismantled and stored in the old potato processing plant that had been converted several years ago to an open warehouse now used mostly for storing floats and other parade items.

Callie had made her apologies to her neighbors who'd bounced off the potato float, to the kids in the marching band she'd disrupted, to Mr. Harwood—their director—and to everyone and anyone who she thought might need an apology. She was sure there would be a write-up in the local paper about her fiasco, but that was nothing new to her. She'd been in the local paper several times in her life for mainly the same type of disorderly thing, except, of course, when she was crowned Miss Russet. Then it was all praise all the time.

*Fickle townsfolk...how soon they forget.*

The regional rodeo had already begun to gear up at the fairgrounds where Callie would once again be joined by the other Idaho Misses to open the festivities the following night. But tonight it was all about the carnival, great food provided by local and some out-of-town restaurants, and the fireworks, which were sometimes better than the Fourth of July celebration.

Piping hot baked potatoes were free tonight, courtesy of the surrounding farmers and ranchers, and everyone in town seemed to be enjoying the perk. The spuds were individually wrapped in parchment paper and cracked open for convenience. Condiments such as butter and other enhancers were provided. However, most residents preferred their spud plain and treated it like a fine wine, savoring the natural flavors. Callie was more into sour cream and chives on her baker, but she usually relegated that controversial fact to her meals at home.

She had been anxious to share the news of Joel's appearance with her sister, who was the voice of reason, for the most part.

"Who exactly am I spying on again? And by the way, he's one fine cowboy."

"Joel Darwood. *The* Joel Darwood who broke my heart, then poured gasoline on it and set it on fire... and he's about as far away from being a cowboy as I'm a rock star."

Coco peeked around the trees to grab a better look. The sisters were barely a year apart, fifty weeks, to be exact, and had always been as tight as thieves. They'd shared everything except their clothes. At six feet, Coco was the tallest of Callie's three sisters, had a bigger bone structure and sprang every button on any of Callie's shirts she'd ever attempted to wear. She wore her deep chestnut hair extra short so she didn't have to mess with it, mostly wore jeans, boots and a T-shirt, and could ride a horse just about as well as their brother, Carson. She was the type of woman who liked to focus on one thing at a time, and for the past six years that focus had been on becoming the best veterinarian this town had ever seen.

"It can't be. After what he did to you, he wouldn't have the nerve to show his face in this town."

"Maybe we could sic Punky on him."

Coco shared her tiny house in town with Punky, a Yorkie who thought he was a German shepherd. He'd been nursed and raised with a group of shepherds after his own mom had died soon after he was born. Punky conducted himself accordingly, being very protective of Coco, who had found him the loving new mama German shepherd who had treated him as one of her own. Nothing scared Punky, not even the biggest of dogs or a horse, for that matter.

Even now, as Punky waited patiently at the end of a bright red leash, Callie could tell he was on full alert. His ears were perked, and an occasional guttural growl emanated from his tiny body, causing him to shiver in its wake.

"Punky deserves better."

"You're right. Joel's not worthy of Punky's attention, good or bad."

"Are you sure that's really him?" Coco asked. "He looks a lot different than those pictures you sent us from college."

"Absolutely. I know Joel Darwood when I see him. Besides, it's been almost six years. I'm way over him."

Coco gazed back at Callie, giving her one of those *yeah, sure you are* looks. "Then why are we hiding behind this tree? And tell me more about that little mishap in the parade today…which had absolutely nothing to do with your seeing him again."

"I told you, I was simply trying to get a better look to make sure it was him. And besides, you know how stubborn Apple Sammy can be."

"He's not the only one who's stubborn."

Callie ignored the jab. "Do you want to help me with what to say to him or not?" Callie stuck a fist to her hip, anxious to get this whole thing settled. She needed to know why the dirty rotten scoundrel was in Briggs and how long he intended to stay. Coco was not cooperating the way Callie had hoped she would.

"Sure, but only if you're sure you aren't harboring some feelings for the guy."

"Stop it."

"What? I'm just sayin'…"

"And what's that exactly?"

"You said you're over him, and I'm going to take you at your word. But what if he and Sarah broke up and he's come to Briggs to apologize for all the pain he caused you? If I remember correctly, you said he was the only guy you ever loved."

"I was young and naive."

Coco gave Callie a quick eye roll. "Not so young, and you haven't been 'naive' since the tenth grade. Remember Blake Granger?"

Blake Granger was the oldest of the Granger brothers, who had a reputation of being real charmers. Back in high school, kissing one of the Granger boys brought on as much envy from the other girls as kissing a cute celebrity.

"I told you a million times, nothing ever happened between Blake and me other than a few hot kisses.

And stop talking crazy about Joel. Like I could fall for his lying, cheating ways ever again. You above all people know how long it took me to get over him, and I am *so* over him."

"Then where's his wife? Where's Sarah?"

"I don't know, and I don't care. Once his wife's aunt Polly left town, no one really kept up on her family. Only that the Double S Ranch has fallen into disrepair, but other than that, there hasn't been any gossip. If his wife isn't here, and if she's anything like she was in college, she's probably hiding out with her current lover. She never could stay loyal to anyone for very long…including me, her best friend."

Callie refused to ever say his wife's name out loud. That hurt still ran deep.

"Do you think he recognized you today?"

Callie had caught the acknowledgment on Joel's face before he turned and walked away that afternoon.

"Unfortunately, yes. The thing is, I don't know what I want to say to him. I mean, I used to know what I wanted to say, but now that he's here, it's like my thoughts are all jumbled up. That's why I pulled you into this. You're good at these kinds of things. What would you say?"

Coco glanced back, then casually leaned against a tree and folded her arms across her chest. "Well, my irate sister, you should've asked me sooner, 'cause that lyin', cheatin', counterfeit cowboy is heading our way."

JOEL HAD SPOTTED Callaghan standing behind the aspen trees almost as soon as she and her friend had arrived. He'd spent the entire afternoon thinking about what he would say to her if and when they bumped into each other today, but so far he hadn't come up with a single thing that sounded the least bit intelligent.

The thing was, he was tired of waiting for Callaghan to come to him. She'd been standing behind the trees for the better part of a half hour, with her friend doing all the spying, and frankly he'd reached his limit. Never mind the tiny slip of a dog that seemed to growl and bark at him whenever he looked their way.

"Where are you going, Daddy?" Emma asked as Joel eased himself up off the blanket they shared with Aunt Polly on the expanse of lawn just on the other side of the small outdoor rodeo arena. The town's fairgrounds were a mix of landscapes conducive to all sorts of events, from the arena with the surrounding bleachers to the blacktop area where all the food stands had been set up, to the grassy part suitable for picnics or waiting around for a fireworks display.

"You stay here with Auntie Polly. I've got someone I need to talk to."

"Okay, but don't take too long. You don't want to miss the fireworks!" Emma warned as she finished off what had to be the biggest puff of cotton candy he'd ever seen. He was sure she wouldn't sleep for the next week from so much sugar, but he just couldn't deny her when she'd asked so sweetly if she could have one.

As he walked closer to Callaghan, his heart started racing and he felt a bit twitchy, like he'd swallowed an entire beehive and they now buzzed through his veins. He'd never really given her much thought over the years, and his wife, Sarah, had barely spoken of her except in passing. Right after everything initially went down, Callaghan had seeped into his consciousness several times, but Joel had been a runner in those days, and running away from his thoughts had been something he'd gotten very good at.

Apparently, he'd recently lost that ability along with his ability to essentially ignore his own daughter. Once he let Emma into his heart, everything changed, almost as if he'd switched on his emotions. Now, as Callaghan and her friend—or maybe it was one of her sisters, he couldn't be sure; he'd only seen pictures of her family— stepped out from behind the trees, English seemed to be a foreign language. His words were all messed up and the only phrase that came to mind was, *get the heck out of here!*

As soon as he came within a couple feet of Callaghan, their silly little dog bared its teeth and growled, as if it was about to do some major damage if Joel didn't curb his ways.

"That dog seems a bit angry," Joel said to the tall woman holding the leash. Facially, she resembled Callaghan, even though size-wise, they were nothing alike.

"He can sense danger," the woman warned, gripping the leash as if she were trying to control a Great Dane or a retriever.

"I'm far from dangerous," Joel told her, trying to make light of the crazy situation.

"Oh, I wouldn't say that," Callaghan countered. "I've been at the receiving end of some of your harsher treatment."

He chose to ignore her barb. "It's been a while, Callaghan. Time has been good to you." Seeing her up close only made the knot in his stomach tighten.

She'd grown a lot more beautiful with time, if that was even possible. She took his breath away.

"I'd return the compliment if I thought for one minute you meant it."

The delusional pooch let out a mouthful of yappy barks. Joel ignored it.

"I'll just leave you two alone," the woman said, her voice deep and husky.

"Please don't leave on my account," Joel told her. "I won't be staying long."

"Why not?" Callaghan asked. "And by the way, I go by Callie now, and this is my sister Coco."

"Nice to meet you," Joel told her, putting out his hand as a gesture of friendship, only she didn't take it.

"I should go," she said, as Joel quickly turned toward Callaghan, feeling about as awkward as a chicken that had walked into a fox den.

The women hugged, then Coco began to walk away, but not before the little dog bared its teeth once more.

Joel chuckled at its spunk. "I don't think that dog likes me."

"He's just emulating my feelings," Callaghan said.

"Ouch!" Joel jerked his head as if he'd been slapped.

Callaghan or Callie wasn't amused.

"What are you doing here, Joel?"

"I'm living in Briggs now, with Sarah's aunt Polly. We're fixing up the Double S Ranch. It needs a load of work, but with a little elbow grease, it's coming along." He knew the work on the ranch was much more than he'd anticipated or knew how to fix, but he didn't like to admit it out loud.

He shifted his hat on his head.

Joel wasn't used to wearing a cowboy hat. The thing weighed heavy on his head and caused him to want to adjust it all the time. Plus, his feet hurt from the new boots he'd decided to wear and he didn't particularly like the pinch of the belt he wore, let alone the buckle that poked him in the stomach every time he bent over.

Truth be told, he was about as uncomfortable in his cowboy getup as a cat in a bucket of water.

"Takes a lot of grit for you guys to show up in Briggs and want to settle down here after all that's happened."

She wrapped her arms across her chest and began pacing just as the first spray of sparkling lights exploded in the sky behind her. He could tell she was saying something, but he couldn't quite make it out over the noise coming from the rapid fire of the fireworks display.

Just as well, the look on her face as she spoke told him she wasn't praising his decision to move to Briggs. No warm and fuzzy for him. No welcome mat or welcome anything. Instead, she seemed to be reciting the riot act, which he deserved, but was glad he couldn't hear.

There was a break in the action so Joel tried to jump in and tell her she was wasting her breath. "Callie, I'm afraid…"

But she cut him off before he could get a full sentence out.

"You should be afraid…" she said, and went on with her muffled tirade.

She finished at almost the exact same time the last

of the fireworks burst in the sky, causing a visceral reaction in him as he remembered another time when they'd watched fireworks together, naked, from the tiny deck outside his apartment off campus. They'd just finished making love when the Fourth of July fireworks had started at the local stadium. She had been hesitant to step out on the deck without even a blanket to cover her body, but Joel had assured her no one was around...until they spotted Old Man Greely peering at her from across the courtyard.

Joel immediately stood in front of her, but by then, Callaghan told him it was too late, so instead she twirled around a few times and danced back inside, undoubtedly giving Mr. Greely the time of his life.

"I'm sure I deserve everything you just said and possibly more," Joel told her, glad he hadn't been able to hear any of it.

"That's your answer?" Her shoulders went down as she shuffled her feet.

"What was the question?"

"What are you doing here, Joel?"

"Like I said, I'm living here now, settling in with Polly Sloan and my little girl, Emma."

"And where's that wife of yours? Oh, wait, don't tell me. She's dumped you for another man. Maybe there is karma in this world after all."

Her comment sliced through his heart, pulling the last breath out of his soul. He assumed... He never suspected for a moment... In a small town like this where news had to travel like greased lightning, it didn't seem possible that she didn't know the truth about what happened to Sarah.

His stomach clenched. "I assumed you knew, Callie. I never for a moment thought you..."

"What? Heard that your wife ran out on you? No. I didn't know, but your showing up here without her can only mean one thing. She left you with a child to raise while she went off with another guy. Is that about right?"

He knew Callaghan well enough to see that hidden under all her bravado, she was still hurting. He didn't know quite how to tell her what had happened to Sarah, how to break it to her gently. He decided instead to simply come out and say it.

"Callie, Sarah died six months ago in a small plane accident. I thought you knew. I'm so sorry."

IT FELT AS if someone had punched Callie in the stomach and forced out all the air in her lungs. She took in a deep, ragged breath. Her eyes instantly reflected her emotion. She tried to control the tears, but it seemed impossible to do.

"I had no idea, Joel. I'm so sorry. What happened?"

As Joel sucked in a breath to answer her question, a blond-haired little girl, with those same sky blue eyes that Joel had, with traces of pink cotton candy on her cheeks, appeared behind him, running full out.

"Daddy! Daddy! Did you see the fireworks? Weren't they beautiful, Daddy? Which ones did you like best? I liked the great big red ones that burst into spinning stars. Those were my favorite. You should've come back, Daddy. We waited for you, but you didn't come back like you promised."

Joel ignored all her questions and instead swooped the child up in his arms and settled her on his hip.

"I'm sorry, kitten, but I'd like you to meet someone I knew a long time ago."

The child wrapped her arms around her dad's neck and nestled her head on his shoulder. "I don't want to meet anybody, Daddy. I just want to go home with you and Auntie Polly."

Callie suddenly felt awkward and out of place. Obviously, she was the intruder in this child's world.

"That's not very nice, Emma," Joel whispered to his daughter. "I taught you better than that. Where are your manners?"

"I'm tired, Daddy. I want to go home." She balled up her hands and rubbed her tearful eyes. Callie couldn't tell if her fatigue was genuine or if she was trying to manipulate her dad. Either way, Callie wanted the awkward meeting to end.

"It's okay," Callie told him, not wanting to intrude on Joel and his child.

"I apologize," Joel told Callie. "She's usually not like this."

"I'm sure it's been a long day for her…for me, too. I'll be heading home soon, as well."

"See, Daddy, even the lady wants to go home."

"Okay, baby," Joel said as he rubbed Emma's back. "But first could you at least say hello to the nice lady? Her name is Callie and she knew your mommy when she was a little girl."

Emma slowly turned toward Callie as she twirled a thick strand of her golden hair between her fingers.

Callie blinked a couple times, trying to take in what she was seeing. Little Emma looked exactly like her mom, down to the dimpled chin and the way her hair curled in little coils around her face. She even played with her hair exactly like her mom had. The vision brought back the good memories of Sarah. The memories Callie had locked away and never wanted to think about again.

"You knew my mommy?" Emma asked in between staggered hiccups.

Callie could hardly speak as she stared at Sarah's child. The resemblance was striking. "Yes, we used to play together at Aunt Polly's house."

"Aunt Polly said she was going to teach me how to ride a horse. Do you know how to ride a horse?"

But Callie suddenly felt tongue-tied, especially after her exhibition that afternoon.

Joel answered for her. "She sure does, kitten. She rode a horse in the parade today."

Emma pushed herself up and away from her dad, then stared at Callie as if she was studying her for a moment. Joel pulled a tissue from his pocket, wiped her nose and dabbed at her tears.

Soon a wide grin spread across Emma's cherub face. "Were you the lady who stopped the parade? She was funny." Emma giggled.

"I...um..."

"Callaghan Grant! Well, I'll be. It's so very nice to see you again," Polly Sloan said, her voice cracking with emotion as she walked up to Callie and gave her a tight hug. "Oh, my darling girl, it's been way too long."

Once Callie was surrounded in Polly's love, she could barely control her brewing emotions over the news of Sarah's death. It was one thing to hold a grudge against her former best friend for all those years, but that grudge didn't overshadow how she felt now that she'd learned about Sarah's passing. Callie never wished her any harm; she simply didn't want to ever talk to her again…big difference.

"Joel just told me about Sarah," Callie whispered, trying to keep her voice low enough so Emma wouldn't hear her. "I'm so sorry."

"Thank you, sweetheart. It was a shock to us all."

When they separated, Callie quickly dried her tears using one of the endless supply of tissues that Joel seemed to have in his shirt pocket.

"You'll come over for dinner one of these nights?" Polly offered. "We'd love to have you as our guest. The place still needs a lot of fixing up, but it's coming along."

Callie didn't know what to say. She had always loved Polly like the aunt she never had. Polly was Sarah's mom's older sister, but she might as well have been Callie's mom's sister, as well. She had treated Callie and Sarah as equals.

When she and Sarah were young, they'd spend most of their summers on Polly's ranch. The Snake River ran right through Polly's land, and the beauty of it was never lost on Callie and Sarah. Most of those long summer days were spent playing in or around the river, sometimes fishing with Polly's husband, Daniel. Callie had acquired a love of fishing from Daniel, and even now, when she felt stressed or anxious, a few hours of catch and release acted like a balm on her raw nerves.

But all those good memories happened a long time ago, Callie reminded herself. A lot had changed since then, changes that hurt even more now that she'd met Emma.

"Sure, but can I take a rain check on that invitation?

I have some work I have to do in the next few days. My new job requires a lot of prep time."

"Whenever you're ready, sweetheart. No rush. Besides, like I said, the place needs more time. You might be disappointed if you stopped by before we brought the Double S back to its former glory."

Emma leaned in on her dad's shoulder, still playing with her hair. Joel held her tight against his chest, then he ran a hand over her hair and lovingly kissed his daughter on the top of her head.

Callie couldn't help feeling a mixture of jealousy and profound sorrow as she watched Joel and Emma together. There was a time in her life when she had wanted nothing more than to have Joel's baby, to be his wife, to raise their children together.

But her best friend had stolen her dream and made it come true for herself instead.

Callie still wanted a houseful of children, more than ever, but she also knew falling in love with the right man, a man who would love her back with the same commitment, was the single most important aspect of a solid relationship and a loving environment to raise those children.

Now, standing this close to Sarah's child and seeing how much that child looked exactly like her mom only made Callie's hurt deepen. Emma should have been her child, not Sarah's.

"Okay, then let's wait. You're living here now, so we have all the time in the world," Callie told her.

"Can we go home now, Daddy?" Callie detected a whine in Emma's voice.

"Sure, baby," Joel cooed.

The child not only looked like her mom, but she seemed to be just as strong-willed.

"We'll see you soon, Callie," Joel told her, then turned and walked away. Polly gave her another quick hug and joined them.

As Callie watched them disappear into the dark night, she knew she had no intention of ever stepping one foot on the Double S Ranch, and she certainly had no intention of ever breaking bread with Joel Darwood, the man she had once loved with all her heart.

JOEL SLIPPED A sleeping Emma into her car seat, made sure Polly was comfortable in the passenger seat and drove his red SUV out of the fairgrounds heading toward home. A full moon led the way on the dark, empty back roads.

"It was nice seeing Callaghan again. Actually it was nice seeing everyone again. I had a great day, and from the looks of it, so did Emma. How about you, Joel?"

Joel knew enough about Polly to recognize when she was fishing for information. They hadn't talked much about his life with Sarah, although he was sure she understood more about it than he'd like her to. He didn't think she knew that he and Callaghan—or Callie... He wasn't sure if he could ever get used to calling her that—had ever dated. Sarah had never been a very forthcoming kind of person. Heck, for the five years they were married he doubted he knew much about her past. It was a revelation to him that she and Callie had spent so much time together during the summer, and even Callie hadn't told him the details of those visits.

For one thing, he'd thought Sarah only visited for

a couple weeks during the summers, but from what Callie had just said, it sounded as if Sarah had spent entire summers with her aunt.

He knew Sarah had grown up as the proverbial latchkey kid. Her mom was always too busy working or out on a date to give her child much attention. She'd had more boyfriends than Sarah could name. None of them were Sarah's dad.

Unfortunately for Sarah, her dad had never been in the picture.

"It wasn't what I'd expected, that's for sure."

"And what was that?"

Joel didn't know how candid he should be with Polly. "For one thing, I didn't expect to see Callaghan in the parade. By the way, she likes to be called Callie now."

"Callie it is. I sensed there was something more between you and Callie than just a friendship, if there ever was a friendship. She seemed a little guarded, but that could just be because she was reacting to the news about Sarah. Funny, but I thought everyone would have known by now. That was well over six months ago."

"Apparently the town must be isolated from that kind of news. Plus, don't forget you and Sarah haven't been a part of this town for several years."

"Still, Callie appeared distant, as if she was holding something back…which didn't seem to be the case when she was talking to you. I couldn't make out what she was saying, but she didn't look too happy."

Joel didn't know if now was the time to tell her about their sordid past, but he was trying to be a more honest man, so this seemed like as good a time as any.

"Polly, there's something you should know about Callie and me."

"What's that?" She turned to look at him, and when he glanced her way he couldn't tell if what he was about to say would hurt her or put a strain on their relationship. He didn't want to do either one, but she deserved the truth, at least as much as she needed to know.

He relaxed his tense shoulders. "Callie and I were dating before Sarah and I got together."

Polly didn't respond for what seemed like forever. His stomach lurched as he waited for her response. He tried to concentrate on his driving along the unfamiliar route, hoping Polly would say something to break the horrible silence.

"Did you love Callie?"

He'd had a passion for Callie, a passion that almost consumed him. He couldn't seem to get enough of her, and felt his absolute best when he was in her arms. She made him feel as though he could do anything, conquer anything and be anything he put his mind to.

But had he loved her?

He couldn't have, or when Callie told him what she saw for their future, he wouldn't have run to Sarah. All he'd wanted was some sound advice from Callie's best friend. He never expected it to go any further than that, and when it did, he just let it happen.

Joel hadn't been capable of loving anyone back then, and even now, love still seemed elusive. Oh, sure, he loved Emma, probably more in the last six months than ever before in her life, but true romantic love, the kind that Polly still felt for her late husband,

Daniel... He didn't know if he could ever feel that sort of deep, powerful love for anyone.

"I couldn't love anybody back then, not even myself."

"But you dated her."

"Yes, for almost two years."

"Did you love Sarah?"

The road before him seemed endless, as if it could go on into infinity. As if he knew he couldn't get out of the car until he told Polly the truth.

"She was the mother of my child."

He kept his eyes on the road, a tight grip on the wheel, looking for his turnoff...hoping for his turnoff.

"You didn't answer my question. And believe me, Joel, I won't be offended by your answer as long as you tell me the truth. I don't abide liars of any kind... at least not on the big stuff. Did you love Sarah?"

He took in a sharp snap of air. "I did not."

"Ever?"

"No."

"Did she love you?"

"If she did, she never showed it or told me."

"Then why did you marry her?"

"She was pregnant with my child."

"But why did you marry her?"

"I just couldn't run away. Not from that. If she was going to have the baby, I would always be his or her dad."

"Still, you could have walked. Paid child support and visited on holidays."

He couldn't do that, even back then he couldn't abandon his unborn child and provide Sarah with a reason to consider giving up the baby. Not that he'd

spend a lot of time thinking about it; he'd merely reacted to the situation in the only way he knew how.
But now that he was forced to rehash it with Polly,
he realized it was the one moment in his life that he
was proud of.

"It was the right thing to do," he said, knowing perfectly well he'd never been all-in either as a husband
or a father. Sure, he married Sarah but he never took
up the responsibility reins...until now.

Polly turned back to face the road and he caught
her glistening eyes that gave away her true feelings.
He could only hope she didn't hate him.

"That's our turnoff up ahead," she said, her voice
steady and strong. "It's easy to miss at night, but look
for the dogwood tree that Daniel planted when we
were first married and you'll always find your way
back home."

"Thanks," he told her, knowing full well he was
thanking her not for the directions but for accepting
his answer.

## Chapter Three

The next morning, Joel went right to work on his extensive to-do list.

First order of business was to pick up materials at the local building supply store in town. Polly had given him a list of repairs that needed to be done, in the order of their urgency. Her ranch of seventy-five acres of mostly brush with a view of the Rocky Mountains contained two good-sized pastures where a fork of the Snake River meandered through. Fortunately, the pastures had been perfectly maintained by Wade Porter, who still leased the land, so Polly didn't have to add any kind of upkeep to her long list. Joel had to admit that Wade sure knew his way around ranching, a skill Joel hoped to emulate in the next few months.

The ranch also had one main pipe corral that was divided into several smaller areas, two outbuildings, one stable that could house ten horses, the main ranch house, one oversize barn located about fifty feet from the main house, and miles of fencing that required considerable fixing.

The buildings needed everything from a new coat of paint to replacing the electric wiring. Joel thought he could handle everything physical, but anything electric would have to be hired out. He had no intention of electrocuting himself while trying to replace a blown fuse. He knew his limits...at least he'd convinced himself that he did.

Now that summer was winding down, the main ranch house took the highest priority on the list, especially the roof. Several of the tiles had either blown off or were too decayed to save. Polly was sure the house wouldn't make it through another rainstorm without leaking, so Joel had taken it upon himself to climb up there and assess the damage. Not that he knew what he was looking for, but he assured himself that he would learn.

Polly had tried to hire a professional team to fix the roof or at the very least, Wade Porter, the resident jack-of-all-trades. Along with maintaining the pastures, he had kept the buildings from falling into complete ruin. Unfortunately, any major work had been put off into the distant future when Polly could make more money.

She never did.

Now the distant future had arrived and Joel had taken up the challenge.

Even though he'd added his nest egg to the pot, money was still tight until they could get more horses to board and buy a few head of cattle to raise. In the meantime, Joel decided to tackle as many projects as he could on his own. He'd spent the last three evenings watching home repair videos on YouTube, taking notes and practicing his nail-pounding skills on a board out in the barn. He was certain he had this roof repair project under control. He'd already fixed the clogged sinks in each of the bathrooms, rehung a couple doors and replaced a few loose floorboards in the living room…all with the help of online videos. He felt certain that fixing the roof would be just as easy.

Besides, physical work would keep his mind off of Callie Grant. After being that close to her the previous night and allowing some of his old feelings for her to bubble to the surface he'd been temporarily thrown off course.

Not anymore. He'd awoken with new resolve. Physical labor would keep his emotions in check and his mind occupied with something other than the softness of Callie's lips or the smell of her hair.

If he was going to make it in this town, Callie Grant had to once again fade from his consciousness and be relegated to his past…exactly where she belonged.

He only hoped he'd be able to avoid her during his many errands into town, which is why he'd left the ranch early, in order to gather up all his supplies and be back on the road within the first half hour after the store opened.

Twenty minutes after leaving the ranch, Joel drove up Main Street like he had several times before, only this time he knew the location of most of the shops. Holy Rollers bakery sat on the corner, next to Galaxy Theater, a recently restored movie theater, according to Polly, that now served up wine, coffee, tea and gourmet popcorn. He'd become very familiar with Geppetto's Toy Shop, a staple of Emma's must-visits whenever she drove into town with either Polly or Joel. Deli Lama's, Spud Bank and Moo's Creamery all inhabited the opposite side of the street along with Hess's Department Store, where he'd bought his first pair of cowboy boots.

The town's favorite watering hole seemed to be

Belly Up, a tavern Joel had yet to visit, but was antici-
pating the moment. Perhaps after he finished the roof
he'd drive into town and celebrate. That is if he could
somehow be assured that Callaghan Grant wouldn't
be inside.

Joel parked his SUV behind From the Ground Up
Building Supply Company, turned off the ignition and
made his way inside the now-familiar store, which
seemed to stock everything a person could possibly
need to repair or build almost anything. The store occupied two stories of a well-used, organized space on
the edge of town.

The strong scent of sawdust and paint permeated
the air as Joel made his way inside. The floors were
well-worn, scuffed, wide wooden planks, and most
of the counters and the checkout area still retained
the original wooden designs. Natural light poured in
from the countless windows in the building. One of
the two cash registers hailed from sometime in the
early 1900s, while the other more modern register
was tucked away behind a large basket of local russet
potatoes. The modern credit card scanners had been
placed inside wooden crates that had seen better days.

Joel walked through the roofing section of the
store, occasionally stopping to sort through the various tiles to find the replacements he needed.

"Polly's roof was probably originally put up in
the seventies, if you're looking to match it," a now-
familiar voice said coming from somewhere behind
him. His instincts told him to ignore Callie Grant and
walk right out of the store, but he knew he couldn't
leave without his supplies. Besides, he didn't want
to be downright rude. He reluctantly turned to face

her as she continued to talk tiles. "They keep some older tiles out back for the locals, but your chance of finding the exact match is pretty slim. Did you look out in Polly's barn? Chances are there's some extras stored out there along with extra flooring, paint that was used on the walls and whatever else you might need to repair and replace what's broken. I bet there's even a few matching cabinet doors and some old fence pipe out there, as well."

"Thanks for the tip," Joel told Callie, trying his best not to seem pleased to see her again. She looked different without her tiara, especially now that her hair was pulled back in a ponytail. She wore a peach-colored sundress that made her dark skin glow, and she smelled like apples, or maybe that was just his overactive imagination.

"I'm surprised Polly hadn't mentioned it."

"She did, but the barn is in such bad shape that I didn't think anything could survive out there."

"You'd be surprised. You might want to take a look before you spend good money on something you already have." She took a step back. "Funny, but I never pictured you as a handyman type of guy."

"And I never saw you as a beauty queen. Why didn't you tell me?"

She shrugged. "The subject never came up."

"How would I have ever known to ask?"

"That's just it. You and your friends were from Boise, the big city, while I was from small-town Briggs. I wanted to fit in."

It was the first time Joel ever realized that Callie had been embarrassed about her past, as if growing up in a small town had been something to be ashamed of.

"Goes to show you how much we didn't know about each other. I was jealous about your roots, about your closeness with your family, this town. I never had any of that growing up. I wish I could have seen you in that pageant. How old were you?"

He could tell she didn't want to talk about it. That for some reason, it still embarrassed her.

"Seventeen. And believe me, I was talked into entering, but this, finding you fishing through asphalt roof tiles, well now, that's something to behold. When did you get into roofing?"

He wasn't sure if she was pulling his chain or sincerely wanted to know about his new interest in DIY projects. Either way, he was feeling a little embarrassed himself. "Only recently."

"As in, since you moved onto the Double S Ranch?"

"Yeah, but I've got a good handle on this. Should be an easy fix."

He continued to search through the different-colored tiles, hoping against hope he'd find a match. He'd already loaded his shopping cart with tar paper, something called a flat bar, a good solid hammer, roofing nails, roof cement, a trowel and a staple gun with extra staples. He was set for anything.

She glanced over at his cart and he wanted to snatch it away, but instead he ignored her.

"You might want to ask Hank Marsh about fixing that roof. It's older and will probably require some extra skills. Hank can fix anything, and knows just about everything there is to know about making repairs inside or outside a house, a barn or a stable."

But Joel didn't want Hank's help. He didn't want anyone's help, and he especially didn't want Callie's.

"There's Hank now." She called out his name as the older, white-haired gentleman in the short-sleeved powder blue shirt shuffled by, causing him to stop in his tracks and walk their way. Hank wore a wide grin, round frameless glasses, and sported a thick white mustache. He looked to be in his late sixties or early seventies and about as wizened as a dried fig. From the look on his face, seeing Callie Grant had to be the highlight of his morning.

"Mornin', Miss Grant. That was quite a parade we had yesterday, more fun than any of the parades I've seen in one heck of a long time. Can always depend on the Grant family to stir things up in this here sleepy town. Glad you didn't disappoint."

"It really wasn't my fault… Apple Sammy wouldn't cooperate."

"Uh-huh. What can I do you and this young fella for this morning?"

Joel wondered what other chaos the Grant family had caused in the town. He really wanted to ask, but he also wanted to buy his basket of home improvement paraphernalia and get the heck out of there. "Nothing. Thanks. I'm fine. I know exactly what I need."

"Just hold on a minute. Joel's fixing the ranch house roof on the Double S. I thought maybe you'd have some pointers for him, Hank."

"'Bout time somebody shored up that there property. Been neglected for way too long. That must mean that Polly Sloan is gonna stay put. Heard the news yesterday from Phyllis Gabaur during the parade that the filly was in town, but Phyllis ain't always reliable with her information. Glad this time she was right. Then you must be that young man I've been hearing about."

Hank extended his hand and Joel took it, but that was about as far as he wanted to pursue this conversation.

Polly had warned him that folks in this town liked to know your business…all of your business. Joel wasn't in the mood to spill any details this morning.

"Sorry to hear about your loss, son. Heck of a thing for your mate to pass so young, 'specially since you've got a little one. Glad Polly brought you to this here town. Best therapy in the world for a youngster is to grow up on a ranch." He glanced down at Joel's shopping cart and shook his head. "Mm-mm-mm! You sure aren't gonna be able to fix that old roof with what you got in that there cart. For one thing, are you repairin' a valley leak, a window leak, the vent or the chimney? They each require special consideration. Or are you just replacing the entire roof, which is probably your best bet. That roof ain't been touched for more years than those tiles were made to last. Plus, in my opinion, roofin' is dangerous business, son. Unless you're a professional, I wouldn't advise goin' anywhere near it. Might slide off and break your neck."

"No worries there. I know exactly what I'm doing." Joel was quick with his rebuttal. Maybe a little too quick. He didn't want to offend Hank. He merely wanted to let Hank know that he had it covered, so to speak. "I've watched more videos than I can count on the subject."

Joel may have exaggerated his abilities, but he'd watched enough home improvement videos that he felt confident he could save himself and Polly a lot of money if he did the work himself. After all, how hard could it be to pound in a few nails and line up some precut shingles? He could do it blindfolded.

Hank seemed to choose to ignore Joel's last statement. "As I recall, Polly's departed husband, Daniel, and me put that roof on in the first place. Stored some extra tiles in the old barn of theirs, 'course, after all this time, might be hard to find and those tiles are probably in worse shape than what's up on that old roof. Either way, there's everything you need right here. Just give me a minute to round up your supplies."

"Thanks, but I think I'm good with what I already have in my cart. I'll just add a few more tiles and I should be fine. No need to go out of your way for me."

Hank stared at Joel for a moment, blinked a couple times, then shrugged. "It's your decision, son. You know where to find me if you need anything else. Give Polly my best." Then he turned on his booted heel and shuffled away.

"Videos? Seriously?" Callie said, shaking her head.

Joel resented the negative insinuation. "I know what I'm doing. I've studied this. Got advice from the best."

She chuckled. "Now I get it. You don't want or need any help. You're a changed man. No more help for you, right?"

Joel took offense at her condescending attitude. "This isn't about anything but fixing a darn roof, which I'm completely capable of doing."

"Clearly."

Joel was no longer paying attention to the conversation. Instead, he'd slipped into panic mode. He hadn't watched any videos on fixing a roof around a window, or anywhere else Hank had mentioned. Could repairing those areas be that different? He was no longer so sure. In two or three sentences, Hank had managed to change Joel's roofing confidence into roofing fear.

Still, he decided to push through and made a mental note to look up an assortment of roof repair videos when he got home.

"And you especially don't want any help from *me*," Callie said softly.

She shrugged, then started to walk away. Joel at once realized what she'd just said. "What? No. This has nothing to do with you."

She stopped to face him, the smile gone. "And here I thought we could come to terms and at least be civil to each other now that we're living in the same town."

Joel knew that for now, he didn't want to be near her. Every time he was, his thoughts seemed to get all jumbled up. He could tell she was over him and probably had been for a long time.

And he was over her...or was he?

"Absolutely. I'm all for being civil."

"Really? And not just to me, but to everyone in this town?"

"Of course. It's my home now. I want to fit in with the townfolk or county folk or whatever they're called."

"Well, you could've fooled me, 'cause you just insulted one of the most helpful men I know, and in doing so, you've made it clear that everyday civility isn't on your to-do list. Good luck with that roof, Joel. And for the record the word is townsfolk, which you are now part of, and if you keep that wall up, you'll never fit in."

As she walked away, he hoped there was an online video on how to adjust to small-town living. Because, for the record, he didn't think he would ever "fit in."

# Chapter Four

The next evening the air seemed to spark with excitement as the folks in the stands readied themselves for the opening ceremonies at the annual rodeo. A clown stood in the center of the large arena at the fairgrounds sparring with the announcer, Harry Sweets, owner of the Sweet Spot, a local chocolate shop. Their voices boomed over the sound system, garnering belly laughs from the children who stood to get a better look at the shenanigans. This was a smaller arena and a smaller rodeo. There was no Jumbotron to capture any of the expressions on the riders' faces, and the neon sign that displayed his or her name and score was visible only from the center of the stands. Which explained why the majority of the side seats remained empty. Still, the enthusiasm of both the audience and the riders was as high as any of the bigger events of the Western Days festival.

Callie looked out over a sea of cowboy hats and smiling faces as she and the other Misses prepared to carry the flags out across the arena. Callie's stirrup had been rigged with a flag boot to hold the flag upright and steady. Apple Sammy seemed a little jittery once she secured the heavy flag in place, his ears twitching as he wavered on his hind legs.

"Easy, boy," she said, and firmly patted his long neck. That seemed to settle him, and it settled her, as well. "We're going to do just fine." His head went up, and he whinnied as if he agreed…at least she hoped he agreed. She could never be sure about Apple Sammy's temperament. Most of the time he was as cooperative as a trained pup eager to please, other times…not so much.

Callie's family sat in the stands: her mom and dad, her sisters, Coco, Kenzie, Kayla and Kayla's husband, Jimmy. Plus her brother, Carson, and his wife, Zoe, were there, as well. Carson wouldn't be competing in this year's rodeo. Now that Zoe was pregnant, he didn't want to be on the road. His focus had switched to teaching, and he seemed to be enjoying spending time at the M & M Riding School instead. Callie had always known her brother would settle down once he found the right woman, and Zoe Smart was 100 percent the right woman. She still ran her wedding planning business, but even that had taken a backseat to her pregnancy.

The entourage of Idaho Misses had briefly practiced their entrance earlier, with flags in place, before the crowd had arrived, so Callie felt confident this would go much better than the parade had.

She took a deep breath and slowly let it out, hoping it would calm her nerves, knowing full well it wasn't the anticipation of the ceremony, which, after ten years, she could do in her sleep. Nope, she knew exactly why she couldn't seem to relax. It was the anticipation of seeing Joel again. Not that she expected him to be in the stands, as he'd given her no indication that he would be there, still, she couldn't be sure.

"Is he here?" Nellie Bent asked as she rode up next to Callie who tried her best not to check out the stands for Joel. If he happened to be in the crowd, it would probably be best if she didn't know.

"I don't know." Callie sat back in the saddle, making sure her flag was seated properly.

"Will you be okay this time?"

"Of course I will." Apple Sammy took a couple steps back, then whinnied. Callie patted his neck trying to soothe him, but she knew he could sense her apprehension. She certainly didn't want a repeat of what had happened during the parade.

"Your horse seems a little spooked. Maybe you shouldn't go out. We can shuffle the flags around. Instead of us carrying two Idaho state flags I can take your flag."

Callie carried Old Glory.

"What? No. I don't care if Joel is in the stands. That situation has been resolved."

Nellie Bent seemed to know more about Callie than she should. That would have to stop or the whole town would soon start speculating about Joel and Callie. When the wretched affair first went down, Callie had been careful in keeping all the details within her family. She must have asked them a hundred times to please not tell anyone. Because of that sense of privacy she felt certain no one in town knew what had happened back in college.

"So his name is Joel? Is that the new guy in town, Joel Darwood? He's really cute, a little old, but still cute. I heard he's a widower. That's too bad for his little girl. My mom divorced my dad when I was a kid and I hated it. I can't even imagine what it would have been like if my mom had died."

Her words cut right through Callie. Four years ago, Callie's mom had been diagnosed with breast cancer, a diagnosis no one wants to ever hear. It just about tore Callie apart watching her mom go through all the treatment and surgery. If it wasn't for the strength her family had during that time, she didn't think any of them could have survived it. Her mom pulled through, and has been cancer-free ever since, but the scars of that time would never truly heal. So yes, Callie empathized with little Emma more than she wanted to admit.

"I'm sure it's tough on his daughter, Emma, but Joel seems to be handling her well."

Just then, the Misses received the signal to gallop out into the arena. They moved at a fast trot to the cheers and whistles of the enthusiastic audience. They headed across the full length of the arena, and would turn to their left and trot back in single file at a fast run so the flags would unfurl.

"I know right where he's seated," Nellie said as they took off side by side, filling the arena with the sound of pounding hooves.

"How could you know that?" Callie asked as they headed to the far end of the arena, amazed at Nellie's gossip acumen.

When they were about to make their turn and gallop back, Nellie said, "Because my sister texted me as soon as he sat down. He's sitting close to my older sister Katina, third row center, second seat in from the left."

Callie's first mistake was to quickly gaze up in the

stands to the exact location that Nellie had described. Once she did, she spotted Joel Darwood flanked by Emma and Polly.

Her second mistake came when, for a split second, she lost focus on her riding.

She pulled a little too sharply on the reins, causing Apple Sammy to turn much too quickly. His feet went out from under him and they both went down. She knew in an instant she would hear about this for months to come.

Silence surrounded her as Callie's tiara tumbled off her head and landed in the rich brown earth, covering its sparkly stones with a fine coating of dust. Callie managed to jump off and away from her horse unscathed, the flag remained in the boot. Apple Sammy righted himself as Callie picked up her tiara. She didn't bother to dust it off and put it back on her head. Then she quickly mounted her horse, secured the flag and took off for the open gate where the other Misses waited for her return.

The place erupted with cheers and whistles as she raced across the arena to the relative safety of the waiting area. As the world shot past her in a haze of Old Glory, she made up her mind that as long as Joel Darwood lived in this town, her Misses days were once and for all unequivocally over.

WHEN JOEL HAD seen Callie go down with her horse, he was up on his feet and heading for the arena without giving it a second thought. A fall like that had to cause some major hurt, if not a broken bone. He'd caught that she'd gotten back up and ridden out of the arena, but knowing Callie, that didn't mean she wasn't injured.

The Callie he remembered never liked to admit she'd hurt herself, even that time when she'd split open her thumb on a broken glass. It had taken him most of an afternoon to convince her to let him drive her over to the ER for a couple stitches. In the end, she'd needed six stitches, and never once flinched as she watched the doctor pull the thread through her skin.

Joel had waited on the other side of a metal gate while a male EMT asked questions and checked her out. Callie looked frustrated with the whole procedure as he flashed a light across her eyes, apparently concerned about a concussion. Once he was satisfied that nothing was broken and she didn't have a head injury, a group of people immediately surrounded her. Joel had recognized a few of them from pictures he'd seen of her family. Her parents were there, along with her famous brother, Carson, plus Coco, whom he'd met the previous night, and two other women he assumed were her other sisters. A few other people had shown up, as well, reminding Joel of how much she was loved.

In the end, he backed away from the group, thinking she probably didn't want him in the mix.

Fine. Well, he'd just have to get her out of his head and one way to do that was to get the heck out of there. So he secured a ride back home after the rodeo for Polly and Emma with some friends of Polly's, and he headed out to Belly Up, the tavern in town he'd been wanting to try. Maybe he'd find some peace there, or at least a distraction from the seemingly constant thoughts of Callie he was having.

Once inside, he made his way along the bare, planked wooden floor to the long, mirrored mahogany bar, pulled up a vintage wooden stool and ordered a whiskey neat, with a locally brewed beer chaser. The honky-tonk seemed rather quiet, and Joel suspected that most of the townsfolk were at the arena enjoying the rodeo.

The jukebox played "Tennessee Whiskey" by Chris Stapleton, and the ambiance was exactly what Joel had expected: authentic Old West complete with a large painting of a nude woman lounging on a bright pink chaise. A wisp of white fabric barely covered the important parts.

The bartender, a sizable man well over six feet tall wearing a large cowboy hat and a friendly smile, dropped off his drinks. "You the one livin' on the Double S with Polly?"

"Sure am," Joel told him, feeling somewhat defensive. He had no idea if this mountain of a man would lash out at him for his past sins or welcome him to the town. He was hoping for the latter.

"Heard you've been fixin' the place up."

"You heard right. It's a real challenge, I'll say that much for it."

"Sorry to hear about your wife, Sarah. Only met her a couple times when she was out for the summers. Spunky little thing. Heard you and she have a daughter… Emma?"

Joel nodded as his defensiveness lightened. "Yep. She's a little spitfire, like her mom."

"I'm Milo Gump," the big man said, reaching his brawny hand across the bar. "Proprietor of this here establishment."

"Joel Darwood."

Joel felt a bit reluctant to reach out his battered and scraped hand, but he did it anyway. The big man must have noticed the wince on Joel's face when their hands met, and let go almost immediately.

"Welcome," Milo said, as a friendly smile creased his lips. "Your first drinks are on the house."

"Thanks," Joel told him, truly thankful for the gesture.

"Does that go for me as well?" the familiar voice said from behind Joel as he turned to see Callie. Her clothes were still dusty, and her hair had been pulled back into a ponytail, but she looked to be all in one piece.

"Sure does, sweetheart," Milo said, looking happy to see her. "Your usual?"

"Yes, please," she said, and motioned to the stool next to Joel. "Do you mind?"

"Not at all."

She carefully straddled the stool, obviously in pain, carefully lifting her left arm and resting it on the bar.

"You okay? That was some tumble."

"My ego's in shreds and I've got some bruises, but fortunately nothing's broken or cracked. Haven't fallen off a horse since I was a kid."

Joel drank down his whiskey, then took a couple pulls from his beer, contemplating the situation. When he put the bottle back down on the bar, he held out his scraped hands.

"I've got a few scrapes and bruises myself."

She cringed, then looked away. "Ranch life seems to be taking its toll. Was that from something specific or just general repairs?"

"General repairs and a little ego letting."

Milo came over and put down in front of her a bottle of the same kind of beer that Joel was drinking, then left to take care of another customer at the other end of the bar.

Callie picked up her beer and held it out. "Here's to crushed egos."

They clinked bottles and, for a moment, Joel hoped that maybe she'd softened her anger toward him.

"Callie, look, I just want to say…"

She held up a hand. "Save it. Just because I pulled up a bar stool next to you doesn't mean I've forgiven you. Coco and I were on our way home when I spotted you walking in here. The only reason I stopped in is because I saw you standing on the other side of the fence when the EMTs were checking me out. You looked concerned, and I wanted to assure you that I'm fine and my fall had nothing to do with you."

The statement caught him by surprise.

"I never thought it had…but now that you mention it…did it?"

She drank more of her beer, then placed the bottle back down on the bar a little too hard. "No, it did not," she said, but he had a feeling she wasn't being honest. "I fell because I took the turn too sharply for the weight of the flag. That's all there was to it. Nothing more."

"If you say so."

"I do," she said, staring into his eyes. He stared right back, and in that moment he spotted something else, something she was trying to hide, a deep sadness, maybe for Sarah, or maybe for the hurt he'd caused her so many years ago.

She continued, "And I also wanted to tell you that as long as we're going to have to live in this same small town, I'd rather you never mention any of the details of our relationship to anyone. It's none of their business."

"I assumed everyone already knew about us."

"There's some speculation, but as far as I know, no one knows the facts and I'd like to keep it that way."

He was all for it. "Not a problem."

"Good, and as far as you and I go, the less we see each other, the better. We can't be friends, Joel, not when so much has happened between us."

He wasn't so sure he wanted to agree with that, but just then he didn't seem to have a choice. "Whatever you want, but I'd still like to explain a few things."

"It won't change how I feel."

"Maybe not, but at least you'll know why I acted the way I did."

"Like a complete ass?"

"Callie, I never meant to hurt you."

"Really? That's your excuse?"

"No. I just mean there were circumstances beyond my control."

"Oh, so none of it was your fault. Perfect. You're still the same Joel from college, the guy who could never take responsibility for his actions."

"I'm not saying that."

"It sure sounds like that's exactly what you're saying."

"You've got it all wrong. Just let me explain what happened and why it happened, and if you still hate me, then fine. But at least you'll have heard my side of the story."

She tried to slip off the stool, slowly, as her sister Coco approached. Fortunately, that silly little dog was nowhere around. He could tell Callie was in a lot of pain, and he reached out to help her, but she pulled away.

"I think I already know your side."

"No. You don't. Whatever Sarah told you couldn't have been the truth. She wasn't capable of telling the truth...not even to you."

They stared into each other's eyes, and for a split second he thought she would listen, that she wanted to listen. He had a glimpse of the old Callaghan. The girl he could talk to for hours about his hopes and dreams, the girl who would confide in him, who trusted him with her heart. It was then that he noticed the long scrape on her chin. He knew she was going to really feel that fall in the morning, and wanted to help make sure she didn't do any more damage as she tried to slip off the stool.

He reached out again and this time she allowed him to help her. This time, instead of moving off the stool, she steadied herself on it, as if she was ready to listen.

"We should go," Coco urged. "It's getting late, and you need to lie down."

"You're right," she told her sister, moving slowly away from Joel's touch.

"Let me give you a hand," Coco said, as she took hold of Callie's arm and assisted her off the stool. A grimace flashed over Callie's face for a moment, then it was gone.

"I'm tired. Let's go home," Callie told her as she reached in her pants pocket.

"Callie, please. Let's meet again and talk," Joel said, his voice low and insistent.

She pulled three dollars from her pocket, tossed them on the bar, then turned to Joel. "It's over, Joel. It was over a long time ago. At this point, I'm sure there's nothing you can say that can change that."

Then Coco slid her arm around Callie's waist, and Joel watched as the two women walked out of the bar.

"Seems like you've got your work cut out for you," Milo Gump said from behind the bar.

"And then some," Joel agreed.

He ordered another round.

CALLIE LEANED UP against the headboard, wearing a long-sleeved gray T-shirt and bright pink capri pj bottoms. She still lived at home with her parents, and slept in the same bedroom she'd once shared with Kayla, the youngest of her sisters. Punky dozed on a cushion on a white rocking chair in the corner of the room, next to a window. Her three sisters, Kenzie, Kayla and Coco—all dressed in their own version of the same type of pj's—sat around her on her queen-size bed, while their mom, Mildred, wearing the bright blue fuzzy robe over the matching pj's their dad had given her last Christmas, put down a white tray holding herbal tea and all the fixings, homemade blueberry scones, a thick pad of butter and fresh cream from Bridget's Dairy Farm down the road.

"Mom, I'm fine. Really. You didn't have to go to all this trouble," Callie said while still trying to get comfortable. Her hip still ached despite the mild pain pills she'd taken at the arena. And her upper arm was now beginning to turn blue. Even the scrape on her chin burned.

"You're my daughter. It's what I do," her mom answered, then she pulled a desk chair up closer to the bed and sat down with a sigh.

Callie knew her mom was tired, but she also knew she couldn't rest until she was sure all her peeps were warm and safe.

Kayla, the youngest of Callie's sisters, had decided to spend the night along with her one-year-old son, Hunter, who had only recently started walking. The women in the family always gathered to support one of their own. The sisters, along with their mom, fawned over whichever of them was hurting until that sister or their mom was back on her feet. Falling off of Apple Sammy apparently warranted that reaction.

"You sure know how to get the attention of an audience," Kenzie said, smiling, blue eyes sparkling, curly sable hair clipped on the top of her head, as she poured golden tea into a mug, then broke off a chunk of scone and handed both to Callie. She couldn't wait to take a sip of the hot liquid. Her throat still felt dry, as if she hadn't quite gotten all the dirt out of her mouth from when she hit the ground.

Kenzie, with her no-nonsense attitude, had taken charge of the situation with the paramedics after Callie's fall. She and Coco had made certain they examined her completely, and even then Kenzie had wanted Callie to go to the hospital. Callie refused. She hadn't fallen on her head and nothing was broken, so a trip to the hospital seemed unnecessary.

Still, Callie knew that Kenzie would be sleeping next to her tonight, just to make sure she was breathing.

"I think she had it planned the whole time," Coco teased as she handed her mom a mug of tea with lots of honey, exactly the way she liked it. "Just like she did when she was in second grade and jumped off the swing to get some boy's attention and nearly broke her ankle in the process."

"It was Georgie Marlow and he never even looked over," Callie said. "Believe me, I learned my lesson after that."

"You could've fooled me," Kenzie quipped, then took a big bite of a scone, moaning over the taste. Their mom made the best scones ever. Nothing compared, not even the ones from Holy Rollers in town.

Their mom said, "Darling, you have to admit, it appears as though you're either consciously or unconsciously trying to get Joel Darwood to notice you... despite your telling us you don't want anything to do with him."

"Or why else would you have stopped by Belly Up tonight when you spotted him going inside?" Coco added.

"Traitor," Callie mumbled.

"You followed Joel into Belly Up? Oh, this is bad," Kayla quipped, wearing a sly smirk, as the light caught in her amber-colored eyes. Her shoulder-length blond-streaked hair was pulled back in a ponytail while she took off her makeup with a baby wipe, a beauty trick she swore by.

Callie had hoped Coco would have kept their stop at Belly Up a secret, at least for tonight, but very little was sacred in this family. Even Callie had done her share of ratting out.

Callie took another sip of her tea. It soothed her

tight throat and helped clear her head. "I told you, I was merely trying to thank him for his concern after I fell."

"What concern?" her mom asked.

"He was there, standing on the other side of the fence while the paramedics were taking care of me."

"Are you sure? I never saw him," Kenzie countered.

Callie nodded, and a pain shot up her face from her chin. She sat back and waited until it subsided.

"Take your time, sweetie," Coco told her. "You're going to hurt for a few days. Go easy on yourself. Try to relax and take this."

Coco handed her a little white pill that she'd dumped in her hand from a small container. "It's a pain reliever. It's very mild and will help you sleep."

"Is this something you give to your animals?" Callie asked, trying to give back what she was getting, and smiled.

"No. It's over-the-counter for humans and something I know that works. I've taken it myself."

Callie took the pill with a sip of her tea. Just swallowing the medicine seemed to help. She cupped her now swollen chin with her hand and said, "Believe me, Joel was there. He left right after you guys came over."

"That was big of him." Her mom still held deep resentments for Joel that Callie didn't think she would ever get over. Mess with one of her kids, and you have Mildred Grant to deal with. Forever.

"He did more than Georgie Marlow," Kenzie said as she settled up against the headboard next to Callie, then gently stroked Callie's hair, moving it behind an ear. "Have to give him credit for that."

"Seems to me it all depends on what Callie here thinks about Joel Darwood," their mom said. "Obviously, she doesn't detest him as much as she used to, or she wouldn't be falling all over herself to get him to notice her. With all the riding you've done on this ranch, a spill like that could only mean one thing."

"And what's that?" Callie mumbled, not wanting to move her mouth.

"You know perfectly well what it means."

Callie leaned forward, despite the ache in her hip. "Mom, I told you it doesn't mean anything. I lost focus and didn't compensate for the weight of the flag when I led Apple Sammy in the turn."

"Ah, but why did you lose focus?" Coco asked, taunting Callie. "You've run that flag hundreds of times and have never fallen. What's really going on?"

No way did Callie want to admit she'd just spotted Joel in the stands and the mere sight of him gave her a visceral reaction she couldn't explain.

"Yeah, and what's the real reason why you stopped at Belly Up tonight? 'Cause I'm not buying that you wanted to thank Joel for his concern. There's more to this," Kenzie said while trying to sound sympathetic.

Callie and her sisters had always been close and protective of one another. Back when the whole miserable mess happened between Callie, Sarah and Joel, Callie had decided not to tell them the whole story right away, mostly because she was so hurt by his sleeping with her best friend after what she thought was a silly argument they would resolve. As it turned out, they never resolved anything.

Instead, Joel, who had always been adamant about not wanting to be tied down by marriage and children, couldn't wait to get his brand-new pregnant girlfriend, Callie's traitorous best friend, to the altar.

When Callie finally spilled the truth to her family, Joel had already driven off with Sarah to live what had obviously been a happy life together.

"When I was mad at Jimmy right after we broke up, all I wanted was an apology and for him to tell me he loved me," Kayla said. "Once he did that, I knew we could work it out. Is that it? Are you waiting for an apology from Joel?"

Kayla had kept her own pregnancy a secret for several months, until one night right before Christmas during their dad's birthday party, when Jimmy had come calling to profess his undying love and apologize for any wrongdoing on his part.

"It's going to take more than an apology, and, well, to be honest," Callie admitted, "I don't know what I want from Joel Darwood. He wants to give me his version of what happened."

"You mean you've never heard his version?" their mom asked, sitting up in her chair, blue eyes peering over the reading glasses perched on the tip of her nose, graying hair pulled up on top of her head with a clip, just like Kenzie's.

Callie nodded. "I didn't want to talk to him back then. I saw no reason for it. Sarah told me everything I needed to know, and besides, he never tried to contact me."

"And you believed her?" Kayla asked, sounding incredulous. "But you always knew Sarah lied."

"Not to me…at least I never thought she had."

"And what do you think now, sweetheart? Now that you can look back and see Sarah for who she was…

what do you think of what she told you now?" Her mom had a way with using her words to make Callie see the true meaning behind them.

"Now I really don't know what to think."

"That sounds promising," Coco said. "For the past six years we've watched you essentially lock your heart away and throw away the key. You've rarely dated, even when we've come up with some pretty good candidates."

"Oh, like that Garrison guy with the braces and bad breath? Or maybe I should have stuck it out with Billy-Bob from Jackson who had an unusually close relationship with his pet cow?"

Her sisters chuckled and agreed. "You had to give him credit. At least Brenda was a blue-ribbon cow," Kenzie teased. "Besides, I had no idea the guy was so into his cow. He seemed normal when I met him at the bovine auction."

"How about Mike Pyke? He seemed like a normal, nice guy," Kayla offered.

"He was if I wanted to date someone who's twenty years older than me."

"What does age have to do with true love?" Kayla asked.

"Nothing, and if I was in my late forties, I might've been all over him. But I'm in my late twenties. Besides, he's just not for me."

"I think you need to hear what Joel has to say. It might clear things up for you," Kenzie said.

Callie yawned, deciding her sister was probably right. "I asked Joel to keep his distance."

"In terms of the big picture, maybe you want to reconsider that idea," Kayla said.

"Don't be ridiculous. Why would I want to do that?"

Kenzie raised an eyebrow. "To get to the truth."

"How do I know I can trust him?"

"You don't, but you can at least listen to what he has to say," Coco said.

Their mom put her mug down on the tray a little too hard. Everyone went quiet. They knew their mom's ways, and when she wanted the floor, she usually barged in and took it.

"Joel Darwood hurt my Callie, and there isn't anything that can change that…but, considering he's now dedicated himself to being a good father for his little girl, who recently lost her mother, and considering he's working hard on fixing up Polly's place, *and* considering he wants to tell his side of the story, I say, as a family, we should give Joel Darwood the benefit of the doubt…at least until he proves himself one way or another."

Punky suddenly sprang to life, let out a couple barks, then turned around in a circle and plopped back down on the cushion, closed his eyes and exhaled a raspy, satisfied breath. Everyone laughed at the silly little dog but Callie.

She could barely keep her eyes open.

"I agree. One way or another," she muttered under her breath, then sank down on her pillow, closed her eyes and fell into a deep sleep.

## Chapter Five

"Damn!" Joel yelled after pounding his thumb with the hammer for the second time. He shook his hand, then sucked on his throbbing thumb for a few seconds, but the pain didn't subside.

For three days straight, at least three or four times a day, he'd played the YouTube video on his laptop that had depicted a couple guys making repairs to an asphalt-shingled roof, one that was much like the roof he was trying his best to restore. He thought he had the process down, but apparently pounding in a nail was proving to be more difficult than he'd anticipated. He couldn't understand what the problem was. He'd hung his share of pictures in his life, so he knew how to pound in a darn nail...or so he'd thought until he began trying to strike several roof nails in a row.

Evidently roof repair was much different than room decorating.

For one thing, the constant worry of losing his balance, tumbling off and breaking several bones occupied most of his brainpower, not to mention the fact that every time he mindlessly put something down, it would slide off the roof and he'd have to make a trip up and down the ladder to retrieve it.

The one good thing in all of this was that he'd had the foresight to warn Polly to stay inside and keep Emma with her. There was no telling what might slide off the roof next.

He wondered how he'd survived until now. Was he so citified that even the most rudimentary tasks on this ranch would prove impossible? And why hadn't his father ever taught him how to repair stuff? Wasn't it a father's duty to teach his only son how to drive a stupid nail into a board?

Apparently, not for his father.

In thinking about it, Joel doubted his dad knew anything about repairing anything. Never once had he seen his dad use even a glue stick. The man had been consumed with making his company work, and even now, after turning "his baby" into the premier accounting firm in all of Boise, he rarely took a vacation, and had never taken a day off except when he'd had his gallbladder removed. Even then, he was back in the office before he'd fully recovered. His mom was the same way, all work.

When Emma was born, they'd sent flowers and even though they lived only a few miles away, they didn't stop by to see her until she was almost a week old. After that, if Joel didn't bring Emma to them, they'd never see her. Joel had blamed their behavior on the fact that they openly didn't like Sarah, but he'd known in his heart that his parents simply didn't want to make the time...just as they'd never made the time for him.

Joel felt proud of the fact that he'd taken the steps to change that cycle, and decided right then and there that he'd make the time to teach Emma all about repairing things…just as soon as he learned.

"How's it going up there?" Wade Porter called up with that dubious tone of his. Joel wanted no part of Wade's brand of help. He felt certain Wade wouldn't merely help, he'd take over while Joel watched from the sidelines, hoping to one day grow up and be just like Wade Porter, a true cowboy. Just because the guy was born with his spurs on and a hammer in his hand was no excuse for him to be so darn helpful all the time. Joel was determined not to be the guy he'd always been: letting someone else do his dirty work. Fixing things on the ranch was Joel's job and, in time, he would learn how to fix anything he put his mind to. At the moment, his mind was taxed with repairing the roof.

"Fine. It's going just fine. Like I said, you don't have to stick around," Joel yelled back as he grabbed another set of asphalt tiles and held them in place over the tar paper he'd covered with heavy-duty roof cement. He picked up his trusty hammer, lined up another nail he'd pulled out from between his lips, and got ready to pound it into submission. "I've got this."

For his entire life he'd done a rotten job of taking on any kind of responsibility, and had allowed his dad to bail him out whenever he got into trouble. It was a wonder he ever made it through college.

Well, not anymore. This was the new Joel Darwood: dependable, loyal, a hard worker, a cowboy who could fix anything…including one *dang* leaky roof.

He whacked at the nail with all his might and caught the tip of his index finger. This time he stifled the rush of cusswords that waited on the tip of his tongue to explode from his mouth. He grimaced and tightened his lips as throbbing pain shot through him. He immediately dropped the hammer with a loud thud, then watched as it slid toward the edge. He barely caught it as he sprawled out flat against the roof so he wouldn't topple off in the process.

"Not a problem. I'm here to help if you need anything. Just give me a holler." Wade shouted over what had to be a thunderous clatter coming from up on the roof. Joel was grateful Wade couldn't see him as he lay there, spread out across the roof like some bug that had landed with a splat. The rough tiles scratched his face and hands as he held on to a loose set that he'd pulled up earlier with his trusty new flat bar. He knew the tiles wouldn't hold him for long, but moving seemed perilous.

*"I'm here to help...just give me a holler,"* Joel mimicked under his breath, scraping his hands as he cautiously crawled back to his safe spot higher up on the roof.

"Will do!" Joel yelled back down with absolutely no intention of *ever* asking Wade Porter for help.

He'd rather eat dirt.

Everything slowed down in that instant as he felt himself lose all control, and he began a slow descent down the side of the roof. It was then that he heard the roar of Wade's muscle truck as Joel tried his best to grab hold of the loose and rusty gutters that surrounded the roof.

The sound of metal weakening then separating from its anchor sent a chill up Joel's spine as he desperately tried to hold on. Then in the next heartbeat, he was free-falling right onto the flat bed of Wade Porter's pickup.

Fortunately, Wade's truck bed was loaded down with bales of soft, pliable hay. Joel landed safely, rolled over a couple times with the momentum, then he tumbled out of the back of the truck and landed on the hard ground right on his butt.

Joel jumped up as if on a spring. "I'm good. No need to worry. All good. Perfect, even."

"You sure?" Wade said from inside his cab, one foot on the ground, ready to assist in any way he could.

Joel dusted himself off and pulled the stick of hay out of his mouth along with the one tickling his ear. "Perfect! Going in the house for a spell. Have me some grub. I'll call you if I need anything."

"Suit yourself." Wade lifted an eyebrow, grinned, then slipped back into his truck, slammed the door and drove off, giving Joel a backhanded wave out the driver's window.

When Wade was out of sight, Joel crossed his legs and sat with an inflexible thud on the ground, completely shaken from his ordeal. His shoulder hurt, his hands were scraped and bleeding, his thumb and index finger had begun to swell, his right butt cheek ached and his ego was massively bruised.

A FULL WEEK had gone by since Callie's tumble at the rodeo, and she was almost back to her old self. Her left hip still ached, and she couldn't quite lift her left arm overhead without wincing, but other than that, and the occasional ribbing she had to endure from her family, she was healing just fine, thank you very much.

She had looked forward to this moment for months, her very first day of teaching, and relished the fact that this class was a bit smaller than usual. It would give her more time to focus on each student individually. For the next nine months, give or take a few weeks off for holidays and breaks, Callie would be consumed with teaching thirteen kindergarten students the basics.

She knew most of the children coming into class from seeing them in town, or from growing up with their parents. There were only a few children who were strangers to her, but she was sure she would find a way to make them all feel welcome. She'd fine-tuned her curriculum and felt it now encompassed all the essentials: language arts, science, mathematics and social studies. Each category was filled with fun things to learn, and Callie couldn't wait to get started.

When she'd heard that Miss Sargent would be retiring, she jumped at the chance to take her place. Callie loved kids—and they seemed to love her—and teaching kindergarten felt like a dream come true. If she couldn't have a whole houseful of kids of her own, at least not yet, having a classroom-full seemed like the best alternative.

She'd arrived early that morning, wanting to make sure her classroom looked inviting to the students, knowing perfectly well that for some children this would be the first time they'd be away from their parents and siblings. It could be a traumatic experience for them, so she'd decided to follow in Miss Sargent's footsteps and adopt a few live pets. She'd brought in two goldfish, Erma and Fred; two turtles, James and Nathan; and two Holland lop-eared bunnies, Wheezy and Squeezy, whom she'd first met in the parade on the 4-H float before her…well…misfortune while riding Apple Sammy.

Callie bought the bunnies precisely because they had been taught to hop over hurdles. She decided her class could enter them in the annual Bunny Hop Contest during the Hearts, Hops and Chocolate festival in February. Plus, the weekly training exercises for the bunnies would teach her students how to reach long-term goals.

Briggs Elementary School only catered to kindergarten through third grade, and if Callie knew children at all, she knew that five- to nine-year-olds, for the most part, were sweet and gentle with animals, at least that was her hope.

"I'm Becky Arlington," the tall five-year-old said. She'd arrived a full twenty minutes before class began, and stood almost hidden behind her mom, Jane, a subdued woman Callie had known since they were in first grade together. Jane had always been quiet, and her daughter matched her temperament.

"Sorry we're so early, but Becky was a little apprehensive of what the classroom would be like."

"We're going to have so much fun." Callie reached out her hand for Becky. "I'm sure you're going to like it here, Becky. Come with me, and I'll show you our turtles and our goldfish, and we even have two rabbits."

As soon as Becky heard about the rabbit, she took Callie's hand. The child wore a bright green dress and dark blue sneakers. Her thick brown hair was made up in two braids that ran the length of her dress, exactly the same hairdo Jane had had at her age.

Callie wondered what her own child would be like on her first day of school…if she ever had one.

The rabbit were kept outside in the bunny hutch she'd bought at From the Ground Up the day she'd met Joel there. The hutch, which was wired for heat, sat right outside the back door, which led to the school yard and was sheltered from wind and rain by the overhang on the roof.

Once Becky held a bunny, her shyness seemed to dissipate and by the time the rest of the students arrived, everyone seemed to be making friends, even little Frankie Carlton, whose voice was as deep as a bullfrog's. He chuckled with the rest of his classmates when the bunnies did something silly.

The bell was still five minutes from ringing as Callie prepared to shore up the group on a large, round, deep blue rug with stars and moons that she'd brought from home. She intended to usher her peeps in a half circle in front of her so everyone sat together on the rug and could get to know one another better.

As she began to lead some of her students to the rug, another student entered the room holding on to her father's hand.

"Got room for one more?" Joel asked, looking almost as surprised as Callie felt. Being so preoccupied with her prep work and setting up the classroom, it hadn't occurred to Callie that Emma might be in her class. If she'd taken a moment to pause and count the years since Sarah and Joel left her in their blissful marital dust, she would've known Emma had to be the perfect age for kindergarten…her kindergarten.

Callie sucked up her swirling emotions and said, "Always room for one more."

She quickly walked over to her desk and picked up the roster with her left hand, momentarily forgetting about the pain it would cause. She cringed, pulled her arm back and reached for it again with her right hand, thinking perhaps she'd missed Emma's name. "Are you registered? I don't see Emma's name, and if she's not on the roster…"

"Sorry, there was so much to do on the ranch that just yesterday I came up for air and realized I hadn't enrolled Emma in kindergarten. Polly reminded me weeks ago, but I kept putting it off." He handed her the official document that made Emma's presence legal, then he whispered, "She's a little apprehensive about being here."

Emma hid behind her dad, not wanting to let go of his hand.

"Aren't we all?" Callie teased, getting a smile out of Joel. She took in a deep breath and slowly let it out, trying to calm her nerves that were already frayed over it being her own first day. She couldn't imagine how this situation could get much worse.

She looked over at Emma, wanting to help her to relax. "It's so nice to see you again, Emma. Want to know a secret?"

Emma stared up at Callie, her big blue eyes moist with fear. Still, she managed a little nod.

"Everybody is a little scared to be here today, even me. First days at school are always a bit frightening."

Emma looked around the room. Most of the children were already sitting on the rug, waiting for Callie to start the class. "Nobody else looks scared."

"That's because they've already met some of the

other children, and they've met our new group of critters, as well."

"What kind of critters?" Emma came out from behind her father's legs.

"We have a couple goldfish, two turtles and two bunnies that all need our care. Would you like to meet them?"

Emma nodded.

"Then you'll have to come with me, and say goodbye to your daddy. But he'll be back to pick you up when the class is over." She glanced up at Joel for approval. He nodded. Callie held out her hand for Emma, who wore a small, bright yellow backpack over her gray tee with the pink ruffle around the collar, matching knit leggings and well-worn brown cowgirl boots.

"You can put your backpack in one of the empty cubbies against the wall," Callie told her, pointing to the white wooden bookcase on the far wall. Emma spotted it, but didn't seem to be in a hurry to drop off her backpack. Callie knew that it took a while for some children to let go of anything they brought from home. It meant they were staying, and at the moment Emma still looked unconvinced.

Joel squatted to Emma's level. "I'll be waiting for you, kitten, right outside that door as soon as the class is over. I promise. You listen to Miss Callie, okay?"

Emma nodded, but gave him a skeptical look. Then she took Callie's hand. "Can I meet the bunnies first?"

"You sure can."

But before Callie could lead Emma outside, little Frankie Carlton appeared. "Holy moly, Miss Callie. I'll show her." He turned to Emma. "C'mon with me."

Emma glanced back at her dad for approval, which

he gave, then she followed Frankie out the back door of the classroom.

"She loves bunnies," Joel said. "Once I get the Double S Ranch up and running again, I'll build her a hutch and buy a couple."

Now that Callie had calmed down from the initial shock of seeing Joel in her classroom, she took a minute to really look at him. His left cheek was bruised and scratched; his hands looked even worse than they had at the bar. Deep scrapes on every knuckle and his thumbnail had to be fifty shades of hurt. And if she wasn't mistaken, she'd noticed a slight limp when he walked in.

"Your hands look worse and is that limp from something new?" She couldn't help the smirk that stretched across her lips.

"Tried to stop a fall off the roof of the ranch house."

"Were you successful?"

"Nope. Landed right on my ego."

"Seems as though that's going around these days. Glad to see there's nothing broken."

He crossed his arms over his chest and tucked his crusty hands out of sight. "I noticed you're having issues with your left arm. Fall off any more horses lately?"

She stood up straighter. "I haven't been riding."

"Probably a smart move."

He shuffled his feet, grimaced and lumbered back to his original stance.

She could tell he was having a rough go of it with the ranch. Plus, she'd heard that Polly had told Marty Bean, owner of Moo's Creamery, just yesterday that Joel was working from sunup to sundown trying to repair as much as he could on the ranch before the weather turned cold. Why he didn't want any help, when from the looks of him he obviously needed it, was way beyond her memory of Joel Darwood. The guy she remembered would never have refused help. Accepting help had been his MO, and once it had been offered, he'd back away from the situation until the helping person had finished the task. Then Joel would step in and take all the credit. There were times when she'd thought his actions were perfectly shameful, when she had insisted he give credit to the other person, and if she pushed it enough, he would do just that...but not very often.

Standing in front of him now, she questioned what she ever saw in that Joel Darwood. But then she was young and naive back in college. The fact that he paid attention to her, and they laughed at the same jokes, and seemingly shared the same view of the world had been enough for her to daydream of one day marrying him.

She was all grown up now. He and Sarah had seen to that, and it took more for her to think about marriage with someone who simply provided a laugh or two. Now she wanted a real man by her side...a real cowboy in her arms.

Could this new Joel Darwood possibly be that kind of man?

The Joel Darwood she'd known had proved that he only cared about himself or he would have never taken up with Sarah after their argument. She'd thought they'd work it out, but before they could talk it over, Sarah had confessed that she and Joel had slept together. And if that wasn't enough of a blow, a few weeks later, Sarah turned up pregnant.

She'd never wanted to hear his side of the story, never thought he'd tell the truth. But now, after what her family had said, she was ready to listen, ready to give him the benefit of the doubt.

What Callie could never figure out was why he married Sarah. Sarah had said it was because they were in love, but Callie could never completely buy it, and Sarah's pregnancy hadn't seemed like a strong enough reason, either. That had been one of the reasons they'd argued the day he'd walked out. He'd been adamant about never wanting children, yet there he was, escorting his little girl to her first day at school. So much had happened. Did she even know this man anymore?

"Here we go," she said, more to herself than to Joel.

He must have sensed her apprehension. He gently touched her hand and said, "You've got this."

A rush of emotion surged through her, as if his touch meant something, as if she still longed for his embrace.

She wondered if her sisters had been right.

Had there been something more in that fall at the rodeo than merely losing focus?

She moved her hand away.

"Thanks," she told him, tossing out a momentary smile, then she turned to her class, wanting to get her first day officially started. The rest of her students seemed to know to gather on the rug and form a semicircle, leaving a section open so she could join them.

Emma sat between Frankie Carlton and Mary Salerno, who welcomed Emma with a hug. Mary's parents and grandparents owned and operated one of the oldest restaurants in town, Hot Tomato, and they knew just about everyone. The Salernos were a warm and affectionate family, always hugging and kissing their more frequent patrons. Apparently, that kind of warmth had been passed on through the generations.

Emma looked adorable, with her sky blue baseball hat, backward, over a mess of curls.

"I'm so excited to be here today. I hope you are, too! Anybody want to tell me why you're happy?"

The children seemed eager to participate in the conversation, each telling her why they liked her class, mostly because of all the critters.

As Callie settled in for the day, she couldn't help but notice when Joel exited the room, closing the door behind him. After she'd left him at Belly Up the other night, she felt confident she'd rarely see him, but having Emma in her class tossed that idea right out on its fat ear.

She now knew she could potentially see him every day.

But now was not the time to think about what that might mean. She had thirteen, no, fourteen children to teach and inspire. She could only hope she would do as good of a job as Miss Sargent had.

As JOEL WALKED back to his SUV in the parking lot, he had second thoughts about leaving Emma in that classroom, and not because he thought she'd bonk someone over the head with a baguette. Polly had prepared a scrambled egg sandwich on soft white bread for Emma's lunch. No crusty bread weapons allowed.

Problem was, he knew how this would end: the

inevitable moment when Emma would do or say something that would cause Callie to set up a serious meeting where she would tell him that his daughter didn't fit in. How Emma was disturbing the class or she'd done any number of unconventional things that could get her expelled.

He hated to think that Callie, of all people, might have to give him the bad news.

What the heck would he do then?

He and Emma had come to the end of their road. This town, this ranch, had to work. His mistake was listening to Polly and registering Emma for kindergarten when there was absolutely no reason why she had to attend, since kindergarten wasn't mandatory in Idaho. She could wait out this year and he could enroll her in first grade next fall. That way he could avoid any and all confrontations with Callie, and perhaps by then, Emma would be much more acquainted with small-town living and would have made some friends.

Joel spun around and headed back to the school. He'd simply unregister Emma and wait until next year. He scolded himself for thinking his daughter was ready for a classroom again when only recently she'd been expelled from what was supposed to be a school designed for more spirited kids.

Nope, he assured himself. This was not the time to stick his vulnerable daughter into a classroom, especially with a woman who still resented him…no matter how sweet she acted toward his daughter.

He walked back through the open front door and made his way down the now-empty hallway to the office and readied himself to pull his daughter out of kindergarten.

## Chapter Six

"Oh, Daddy, Miss Callie is the best teacher ever! We get to play with Wheezy and Squeezy all the time. He's here, Daddy. Wheezy's one of our bunnies. And Frankie said I can sit next to him again tomorrow. Frankie's in my class. He taught me how to feed the bunnies. Did you know bunnies like strawberries and bananas, Daddy? I like strawberries just like Wheezy does."

Emma was so happy Joel thought she might burst. "No, I didn't know that, kitten."

"Yeah, and kale, too. But I don't think I like kale, so don't buy me any, okay?"

"Okay. No kale for you."

"I got to feed Wheezy, Daddy, and I got to hold him for a really long time. But we can't hold him too tight or we might hurt him. We have to be very gentle, Daddy. He likes being held and he likes to jump, too. So does Squeezy, but Wheezy jumps higher. Miss Callie said so. She walked them both around a little track we made, and they jumped over each hurdle. Sometimes Wheezy didn't want to jump and looked silly just sitting there. He made me laugh. He would make you laugh, too, Daddy."

Joel stood in front of the school as parents and children swarmed around him. Sunshine danced off every surface while the deep green grass surrounded him with its sweet scent as if it had been recently cut.

He knelt down on one knee to better talk to his daughter. "Are you trying to tell me you like this school?"

She bobbed her head several times.

"It's superfantabulous, Daddy. I love it. And Miss Callie says I can stay as long as I want. Can I, Daddy? They aren't going to make me leave, are they, Daddy?"

Ironically, the older woman who worked in the office, Mrs. Pearl, had advised him to stop and think for at least twenty-four hours about pulling his daughter out of kindergarten. Thanks to the astute Mrs. Pearl, he'd reconsidered his attempt at sabotaging his daughter's happiness.

"Not a chance, kitten. We live here now. This is your school and will be for a very long time."

Emma reached out, flung those sweet little arms of hers around Joel's neck, and giggled into his shoulder. His heart swelled. He hadn't seen his daughter this happy in months. It took all his fortitude not to well up and blubber like a baby.

"Daddy, can we go home now so I can tell Auntie Polly all about it?"

"We sure can, baby," he told her while he stroked the back of her head and held her tight. He loved his little girl more than he could put into words, and relished moments like this. He'd missed out on so much of her life that he wanted to wallow in her happiness and try to make up for his past mistakes.

"We had fun with Emma today," Callie said from somewhere above him.

He cleared his tight throat, blinked away the tears and stood, taking Emma's hand in his.

She asked, "Can I say goodbye to Mary, Daddy? She's nice."

Emma stared off in the near distance at a girl Emma's age standing alongside a woman who appeared to be her mom, a stylish woman with short-cropped brown hair somewhat hidden under a white cowgirl hat.

"Sure, kitten," Joel told her as she slipped from his grasp and ran to her little friend. "Just stay where I can see you," he shouted.

"I haven't seen her this happy in a long time," Joel told Callie as he watched Emma and Mary run around in circles, giggling.

"She's a smart little girl, Joel. She can read far beyond what we read in class, and from the little bit of math I gave the students today, I have a feeling she's good with numbers, as well."

Joel couldn't take credit for any of that. Sarah had many faults, but she'd made a few feeble attempts at taking the time to teach Emma her numbers, her letters and how to read. Deep down, he knew, in her own way she'd tried to be a good mom, even though she and Joel had always been busy outdoing each other with jobs and friends—and, he later learned, she'd had an assortment of extramarital affairs. Polly had taken up the slack for the most part when it came to Emma's education. Regrettably, because of all their bad behavior, and except for Sarah's intermittent attempts to be a good mom, neither one of them had spent enough quality time with Emma.

"Sarah gets some of the credit for that, but it was Polly who did most of the teaching. Sarah and I were too busy with our own lives to do much."

"You must have had some kind of impact on her. You're all she talks about."

"About how much I wasn't around, no doubt."

Joel knew he deserved Emma's wrath for more or less abandoning her for the better part of her life, but it was still hard to take.

"According to Emma, you read to her every night."

Joel had only recently started reading to Emma, but it wasn't something he had initiated. Polly had been too busy with chores when they first arrived and had asked him to take over for a couple nights. That was more than a month ago. He found that he loved reading to Emma, teaching her the words on the pages and making up their own stories about the pictures.

"I guess I do. She seems to like it."

"I've got news for you. She loves it."

Callie smiled, and all that sunshine that danced around them now seemed to be radiating from her. She had blossomed into a feisty, self-confident and determined woman who seemed to love children, and they loved her.

Plus, drop-dead gorgeous with those almond-shaped eyes, that fine, thin nose, the sultry color of her skin, and full lips that had always sent a shiver through him whenever they kissed. He was happy he had Emma in his life and wouldn't change that for the world, but he deeply regretted walking away from

Callie back in college. Even now, he still believed she deserved a better man than he could ever be.

Callie was the very first teacher who had ever spoken so highly of his daughter. He didn't know if that was due to an built-in fondness she seemed to have for Emma or if it was a genuine acknowledgment of Emma's acumen. Either way, Callie had succeeded in dissolving all the apprehensions he'd had about his daughter being in her class.

"Then I should continue?"

She chuckled. "Absolutely!"

Never in Joel's entire life had he been more pleased about his decision to wait twenty-four hours. Waiting had never been on his radar screen.

He was beginning to finally understand the true meaning of the word.

THE NEXT COUPLE weeks proved to be both exhilarating and frantic for Callie. Wrangling fourteen students and keeping them occupied had proven to be more difficult than she'd anticipated, but she was slowly getting a handle on it. Plus, her fear of something horrible happening whenever she was in Joel's presence had eventually crumbled. She was getting used to seeing him standing out in front of the school, waiting for Emma, leaning on the metal railing, cowboy hat tipped back on his head, jeans and boots dusty from whatever he'd been into before he left the ranch, blue eyes sparkling in the late afternoon sun, looking as if his chest and arm muscles were growing by the day.

"How'd you do in school today, Emma?" he'd ask as soon as he saw his daughter.

"It was fun," Emma would say as she brushed past

him and ran to the sidewalk with her friend to wait for her dad.

Inevitably, Joel would turn to Callie and ask how Emma was doing, or if she was behaving herself.

"She's fine, just fine," Callie would tell him, sometimes stretching the truth a bit.

Most of the time, it was true. Emma shared the toys and played nicely with the other children, but every once in a while, Emma would hoard the toys and not let the other children near whatever she wanted to play with. Or she'd take one of the bunnies and outright lie to the other children. "Miss Callie said that I'm the only one who gets to play with Wheezy today."

Some of the children would cry, while others would report to Callie and she'd have to get tough with Emma. "Emma, you know that's not true. Let's put Wheezy back in his hutch so the other children can pet him."

"No, I don't want to." Then she'd run out into the school yard. Callie would have to go after her and find a way to make her give up poor Wheezy.

Emma could be so challenging that on some days Callie would be at her wit's end.

Still, she persisted in thinking she could break through Emma's bad behavior, and until she did, she decided not to burden Joel with any of it. He had enough going on with the ranch, he didn't need to know about Emma's occasional bad behavior…at least not yet.

Joel and Callie were becoming friends, each being cordial to the other despite the big dark cloud that hung over them. She knew that one day they'd have to discuss their past, but the school yard wasn't exactly the best place.

Now as Callie stood out on the front lawn with Emma, waiting for Joel to pull up at any moment, she wondered if that day would ever come. The man was probably too busy with his ranch to think about mending fences with an old girlfriend he'd long since moved on from.

Callie knew he was focused on the repairs, even finally hiring a mechanic to come out and get the tractor and other equipment up and running again. But he seemed to be stubborn about hiring someone to help with everything else. Which probably accounted for his tardiness today.

"Where's my daddy?" Emma asked, her voice sounding shaky. "I want my daddy to be here now. Where is he?"

"I'm sure he's on his way, Emma, but I can call him if that would make you feel better."

"I want my daddy," Emma said, just before big tears began to fall.

"As soon as I get him on the phone, you can talk to him. Okay?" Callie was careful with how she phrased her sentence and how she comforted Emma. She didn't want Emma to pick up on how she felt, and for that matter, she didn't want Joel to know, either. Still, she couldn't shake the feeling. The more she was around Emma, the more she realized that Emma simply was not the kind of child Callie could relate to.

Emma wiped her tears with her hands and nodded as Callie tapped on Joel's number. She had the contact information for all her students on her phone, just in case there was an accident or for a situation like this.

Joel didn't answer so Callie left a message, which made Emma cry even harder. No way could Callie handle this situation for very long. Try as she may, Emma was inconsolable.

"Nothing worse than a crying child and a parent who ignores his responsibilities," Mr. Crawly, the second-grade teacher, remarked as he walked past Callie. "I'll make note of his tardiness to Mrs. Pearl. I don't know if you're familiar with the latest procedure for this, but if he's late two more times, the child can be suspended. I've seen her dad drop her off, but I don't know his name."

Zeke Crawly was a busybody, a fiftysomething recently divorced man with a perpetual chip on his shoulder. Maybe the chip was from the loss of his wife, or maybe he'd always been that way and his wife had finally had enough. Callie didn't know the answer to that one. Unfortunately, he seemed to have a lot of pull on the school board, and despite her wanting nothing to do with him, in this case, he might have a point.

"Joel Darwood," Callie told him, but as soon as she said his name she wanted to take it back. "But he probably got tied up in something and lost track of time."

"No excuse," Mr. Crawly said, and proceeded past her into the school.

At this point, there was only one thing left for Callie to do. "How 'bout if I drive you home today? Would you like that?"

Emma nodded, hiccupped and attempted to soothe herself. Callie pulled a tissue out of her purse and gently wiped Emma's eyes. "That's better. Now let's get you home. We should be there in no time."

Callie knew that if this was in a bigger city, she'd

have to wait for Joel to contact her, but this was Briggs and in Briggs it was fine for a teacher to give a child a ride home…on occasion…and this was most certainly one of those occasions.

A few minutes later, Callie and Emma were on their way to the Double S Ranch.

"All set?" Callie asked as Emma strapped herself into the backseat of Callie's extended-cab pickup.

"All set," Emma repeated. "My daddy usually picks me up. He's big and strong and…"

Emma rattled on about her dad, how busy he was, the ranch, her classmates, Aunt Polly and anything else that floated into her consciousness. It reminded Callie of a continuous stream of innocuous chatter, much like background music. The kind where you sense it's playing, but you never stop to recognize a song. Nothing is ever distinctive. It merely all blends together in a sort of din that either soothes you or grates on your nerves.

Emma hadn't reached the grating on her nerves point…yet. She was still in the background din category, but Callie felt certain if she had to drive her home on a regular basis, her nerves would soon be raw. She hated how she felt, but she couldn't seem to figure her way out of it, no matter how much she wanted to.

Callie ignored much of what Emma said as they headed up the road toward the Double S Ranch, only occasionally giving her an "uh-huh" or a "that's nice, Emma." Callie didn't consciously try to tune her out; it more or less happened organically whenever the two of them were confined for any length of time. She remembered how Emma's mom had had the gift of gab, and there were times, for Callie's own sanity, when she'd had to ask her to please stop talking for a while.

It struck Callie how similar mothers and daughters were, and she wondered if the similarities were learned, like tying a shoe, or was it genetic, like blue eyes and blond hair. She knew for a fact that she and her own mom shared a love of children and family. All the girls in the Grant family shared a love for good-quality tea, and almost anything baked with sugar and butter, but that was probably more about growing up with their mom's pastries. Everyone in the family, including their dad and Kayla's husband, Jimmy, had a terrible sweet tooth. She didn't think anyone would be accepted into the clan without a love for everything sweet.

The thought made her mouth water for one of her mom's pies…or a scone…or a slice of chocolate cake and a hot cup of tea. She would much rather be enjoying herself with any one of those things while sitting in a rocker on the front porch at home right now rather than driving Emma home.

Joel Darwood would get an earful. That was for sure.

As they approached the turnoff for the Double S Ranch, Callie thought she heard Emma say something about her horses, but by the time her mind clicked in and she registered what Emma was saying it was too late. She'd already made the turn.

Two majestic chestnut-colored horses stood in the middle of the dirt road, directly in front of Callie's moving truck.

Callie yelled as she swerved to the opposite side of the road trying desperately to avoid hitting them. The next thing she knew she was heading for a deep ditch off the narrow shoulder. "Hold on, Emma!"

But Emma was already screaming not to hit her horses as she sobbed in the backseat.

Callie turned the wheel, praying she'd bypass both horses and the steep ravine just off the shoulder. Her hands had a viselike grip on the wheel, and her focus lasered in on her driving. It seemed as though time slowed and her breathing was nonexistent. With some incredible maneuvering, Callie managed to skim the tight, rocky shoulder and miss the horses, which had since run off the opposite side of the road toward the open land that surrounded the Double S.

When Callie finally stopped the truck in a safe spot on a more even part of the shoulder, she jammed the gearshift into Park and switched off the ignition. Then she turned back to Emma expecting the worst. Instead, Emma's eyes were big and round and Callie knew the child could go either way, depending on how the adult reacted. She needed to keep Emma calm, especially since her own emotions were about to explode.

Callie took a deep breath and tried her best not to show any concern over what had just taken place. "Wow, Emma, that was something, wasn't it! Thank you so much for warning me about the horses. That was sure smart of you to tell me about them. You really helped out a lot. When I first took the turn, I didn't see them. Thank you for being that aware!"

At once, Emma seemed to relax; her eyes narrowed and the corners of her mouth went up. "You're welcome," she whispered. "Can we go home now? I want my daddy."

"Absolutely. We should be there in a few minutes."

Emma gently nodded, but Callie could tell the child's emotions were ready to pour out. Heck, Callie's emotions were ready to pour out. It took all her inner strength not to blubber like a baby. When she thought of what could have happened, it gave her a shiver, so she pushed the thought away and reluctantly readied herself to turn over the ignition. Her hands were still shaking as she reached for the key. Not a good sign. She told herself everything was fine. She and Emma were fine. She gulped a couple deep breaths, but she couldn't quite get her body to listen.

"I want my daddy," Emma repeated, her voice a little unstable.

Callie consciously relaxed her tight shoulders and tried to convince herself she felt as steady as a rock.

"Hang in there, Emma. We're almost home."

Callie glanced in the rearview mirror getting ready to start the truck up again and pull out just as she spotted a ranch truck pull up behind her and park.

Joel got out.

She'd never been so happy to see Joel in her entire life.

"You two okay?" Joel shouted as he approached Callie's truck. "Something happen to your truck? It's way too dangerous to pull over on this narrow shoulder. You could've easily driven right over the side and ended up in that ditch."

The last thing Callie needed at the moment was driving lessons from Joel Darwood.

"We're fine," Callie told him, a little miffed at his attitude. "Thank you very much. And I didn't drive into that ditch, as you can see."

Emma instantly started crying as soon as she saw her dad, holding out her arms for him to pick her up. "Oh, Daddy!"

Callie remained inside the cab for a moment longer, trying to brace herself.

Joel reached inside, unbuckled his daughter's seat belt and pulled her into his arms. "What's wrong, kitten?"

Callie wished he'd pull her into his arms, as well. That was the closest she'd ever been to having a major accident. If she had hit those animals, there was no telling what might have happened. She couldn't even think about it without wanting to cry.

Emma continued to sob, but managed to tell her dad how their horses were standing in the road. "Why would they do that, Daddy? Don't they know that the road is for cars and not for horses?"

"I don't know what you're talking about, cupcake. What happened?"

"The horses...they were in the road."

"What horses? I don't see any horses, kitten."

"Our horses, Golden Girl and Rockabilly. They... they were here."

Joel stooped down to talk to Callie, who was still trying to rustle up some calm. "What is she talking about?"

"Two chestnut horses were standing dead center in the road," Callie told him, wondering where the heck they had come from. They were nowhere to be seen now.

"So you ended up here, heading straight for a ditch? Couldn't you simply have driven around them? Or were you going too fast and not paying attention?"

Callie was about to defend herself when Emma said, "But we didn't hit them, Daddy. We almost did, but they ran off instead. I saw the horses before Miss Callie did, and she turned the truck so we could miss hitting them. I was scared, Daddy. Really scared."

He threw Callie a scowl, then started back for his truck. "I've got you now, baby. Everything's going to be okay. I promise."

Callie closed her eyes and tried to relax her tense body, but all she could see were those two beautiful animals staring at her with their big brown eyes.

Of course, Joel's dismissive attitude didn't help her nerves one bit. If anything, he'd succeeded in making her angry that he wasn't more appreciative of her driving skills. She'd reacted on instinct, after years of driving on her parents' ranch avoiding livestock, boulders, downed tree limbs and an assortment of other roadblocks. She'd learned how to maneuver a moving vehicle, and it had all paid off today.

But apparently, Joel didn't see it that way.

Once Emma felt safe in her daddy's arms she stopped crying. Callie could hear him tell his daughter that the horses would be fine, and that they had probably meandered home by now.

Callie wanted to go home. She opened her door and slid out, feeling a bit better, but still weak in the knees.

"I'll be leaving, then," Callie told him, trying to sound as if she wasn't still a quivering mess on the inside. Joel looked pale as he held on to Emma, soothing her as he stroked the back of her head. His normal easygoing demeanor had been replaced by a combination of relief, anger and terror that his daughter might have been in a terrible accident. Callie could understand his mixed emotions, but she didn't appreciate his anger directed at her.

"Your cheek is bleeding," Joel told her, looking concerned.

Callie's hand instinctually went right for the bump on the left side of her face and sure enough, she'd been cut. How it had happened was a complete mystery.

"I'm sure it's just a little scrape. I'll be fine."

He stepped in closer to her. "I'm sorry if I came across a little too aggressive—just upset over what might have happened. Time got away from me and when I went to call you, my phone was dead. Forgot to charge it last night. Thanks for driving Emma home. I know it's out of your way."

"I didn't know what else to do," Callie told him, her stomach shaking.

Joel must have sensed her condition. "You should stop in at the house for a while," he said, his voice softer now. "Let's clean that wound. I have tissues in my truck to stop the bleeding. Polly can tell if you need to see a doctor. She studied to be a nurse when she was young. You can leave your truck here. I'll drive."

For a moment, Callie hesitated, not really sure if she should take him up on his offer, but she couldn't seem to shake the queasy feeling that now engulfed her. Plus her cheek suddenly throbbed.

"C'mon. Besides, I don't think you should drive right now." He reached out and ran his rough hand over her arm. This time, she didn't pull away from his touch, but rather leaned into it, needing his strength, his composure to calm her growing anxiety.

"You're right," she told him, then secured her rig

and headed off to his truck, trying her best not to stumble on the uneven ground.

When they were on their way, Joel said, "Once I get you two up to the house, I'll check on the horses. If they're not in the corral I'll drive back out and look for them. If they ran off toward the ranch, which I think they did because you swerved away from them, toward the shoulder, they'll be fine. The main road is behind them. But what I don't understand is how they got out. I just fixed that corral gate yesterday."

If Joel had been anyone else who lived on a ranch, Callie would have thought that perhaps someone had accidentally left a gate open. But this was Joel Darwood who hadn't yet got the hang of cowboying, and was stubbornly trying to do everything himself. The way she had it figured, he probably fixed the gate after watching a video on the subject that didn't take into account what happened if and when the horses tried to push the gate open.

"I think it's still broken, Daddy. Maybe Wade could fix it next time. Auntie Polly says he's good at fixing things."

Callie smiled, but didn't say a word.

"It doesn't look too bad," Polly said as she swabbed Callie's cheek with a cotton ball soaked in hydrogen peroxide. Joel knew the sting had to burn like crazy, but Callie never flinched. He remembered how she'd told him once that she'd grown up with her mom washing every cut, scrape and scratch with the stuff. Still, it looked painful as the white foam from the peroxide billowed on her cheekbone. "I'm betting you might have cut it with your own fingernail."

Callie held up her hands to check them for blood, and sure enough Polly was right.

"There's blood on my index finger," Callie said, showing the evidence to Polly. "I never even felt it. Plus, I thought I had both hands on the wheel the whole time."

"Things happen so fast in a moving vehicle you don't realize the damage until you come to a stop, and even then sometimes it takes a while. I'm just so thankful you and Emma are okay."

"That's for sure," Callie told her.

Joel could tell Callie was finally relaxing. The shaking had subsided and she seemed to be breathing normally again. He hadn't seen what had happened, but whatever it was, it couldn't have been good. If Callie drove a truck the way she'd been riding a horse lately, he was darn lucky nothing had happened to his little girl.

He didn't think he could survive Emma getting really hurt or worse... He couldn't even go there. It still made him quiver whenever he thought about how Sarah had almost taken Emma with her on that deadly trip. She changed her mind that morning when Polly offered to babysit Emma for the weekend. He may not have paid much attention to Emma before that tragic day, but he always loved her from the moment he first held her in his arms. Emma was the best thing that ever happened to him, and there wasn't anything he wouldn't do to keep her happy and safe.

And that included never trusting anyone other than himself to drive her to and from school. He promised himself he'd never again allow work to distract him.

The good thing in all this was that Emma had been

completely checked out by Polly and had passed inspection with flying colors. She was now busy watching the movie *Frozen* in her room. It was the one thing she turned to whenever she was upset. In the days after her mom died, Emma must have watched it a hundred times. Even Joel knew most of the dialogue and all the words to the songs. In some ways, watching the movie with Emma had been therapeutic for him, as well.

Maybe later he'd watch the movie with Emma once again. He still couldn't quite shake how upset he was over Callie's close call with both the horses and the ditch. He felt certain the whole episode could have been avoided if he'd been driving.

All Joel wanted was for Polly to get Callie fixed up so he could drive her back to her truck. He'd already checked the corral and the horses weren't there, so they had to be on the land somewhere. But to be on the safe side, he called the local sheriff's department to warn them in case those horses wandered out to the main road.

Once he sent Callie on her way, he'd figure out how to round up his horses, bring them home and secure them in the stable this time. Then he'd spend the rest of the evening with his daughter.

"Almost done there, Polly?" Joel asked, hoping to get Callie moving.

"Yes, I should go," Callie said as she stood up, but then couldn't quite take a step. Instead, she plopped back down again.

Joel quickly reached out to steady her, but Polly seemed to have it under control and held Callie in her chair. His heart raced from seeing her stagger like that. Was she hurt more than Polly thought?

"When was the last time you ate something?" Polly asked.

Callie didn't answer right away, as if she was trying to remember. It reminded Joel of their college days when she'd get busy with her work and forget to eat for an entire day. "I know I ate breakfast."

"What time was that?" Polly asked.

"Around six this morning."

"And since then?"

"I must have… No, Frankie's mother stopped by during lunch. He'd gotten sick in class, so she took him home early. He has a sensitive tummy. Then there was Mary's mom, who needed some forms filled out for an after-school program, and…"

"So in other words, you haven't eaten in over ten hours. You're not leaving here until you've had a good solid meal. Let's chat for a while and have a cup of tea first. You and I haven't had a nice long talk since I've been back. We'll catch up while I fix you something to eat."

"That would be nice. Thank you," Callie said, leaning back in the chair.

"I'll go look for our horses and be back as soon as I can," Joel said.

He grabbed his keys off the hook on the wall where he always kept them, slipped his hat on his head and was just about to leave when there was a knock at the door. He opened it and Wade Porter stood in the open doorway.

Directly behind him, Golden Girl and Rockabilly were tied to the railing, looking no worse for wear.

# YOUR PARTICIPATION IS REQUESTED!

Dear Reader,

Since you are a lover of our books – we would like to get to know you!

Inside you will find a short Reader's Survey. Sharing your answers with us will help our editorial staff understand who you are and what activities you enjoy.

To thank you for your participation, we would like to send you 2 books and 2 gifts – **ABSOLUTELY FREE!**

Enjoy your gifts with our appreciation,

*Pam Powers*

**SEE INSIDE FOR READER'S SURVEY**

# For Your Reading Pleasure...

We'll send you 2 books and 2 gifts
**ABSOLUTELY FREE**
just for completing our Reader's Survey!

# YOUR READER'S SURVEY
## "THANK YOU" FREE GIFTS INCLUDE:
- ▶ 2 FREE books
- ▶ 2 lovely surprise gifts

### PLEASE FILL IN THE CIRCLES COMPLETELY TO RESPOND

**1)** What type of fiction books do you enjoy reading? (Check all that apply)
- ○ Suspense/Thrillers   ○ Action/Adventure   ○ Modern-day Romances
- ○ Historical Romance   ○ Humor   ○ Paranormal Romance

**2)** What attracted you most to the last fiction book you purchased on impulse?
- ○ The Title   ○ The Cover   ○ The Author   ○ The Story

**3)** What is usually the greatest influencer when you <u>plan</u> to buy a book?
- ○ Advertising   ○ Referral   ○ Book Review

**4)** How often do you access the internet?
- ○ Daily   ○ Weekly   ○ Monthly   ○ Rarely or never

**5)** How many NEW paperback fiction novels have you purchased in the past 3 months?
- ○ 0 - 2   ○ 3 - 6   ○ 7 or more

## YES! I have completed the Reader's Survey. Please send me the 2 FREE books and 2 FREE gifts (gifts are worth about $10 retail) for which I qualify. I understand that I am under no obligation to purchase any books, as explained on the back of this card.

### 154/354 HDL GLNW

FIRST NAME                    LAST NAME

ADDRESS

APT.#     CITY

STATE/PROV.     ZIP/POSTAL CODE

## READER SERVICE—Here's how it works:

Accepting your 2 free Harlequin® Western Romance books and 2 free gifts (gifts valued at approximately $10.00) places you under no obligation to buy anything. You may keep the books and gifts and return the shipping statement marked "cancel." If you do not cancel, about a month later we'll send you 4 additional books and bill you just $4.99 each in the U.S. or $5.74 each in Canada. That is a savings of at least 12% off the cover price. It's quite a bargain! Shipping and handling is just 50¢ per book in the U.S. and 75¢ per book in Canada.* You may cancel at any time, but if you choose to continue, every month we'll send you 4 more books, which you may either purchase at the discount price plus shipping and handling or return to us and cancel your subscription. *Terms and prices subject to change without notice. Prices do not include applicable taxes. Sales tax applicable in N.Y. Canadian residents will be charged applicable taxes. Offer not valid in Quebec. Books received may not be as shown. All orders subject to approval. Credit or debit balances in a customer's account(s) may be offset by any other outstanding balance owed by or to the customer. Please allow 4 to 6 weeks for delivery. Offer available while quantities last.

▼ If offer card is missing write to: Reader Service, P.O. Box 1867, Buffalo, NY 14240-1867 or visit www.ReaderService.com ▼

BUSINESS REPLY MAIL
FIRST-CLASS MAIL    PERMIT NO. 717    BUFFALO, NY

POSTAGE WILL BE PAID BY ADDRESSEE

READER SERVICE
PO BOX 1867
BUFFALO NY 14240-9952

NO POSTAGE
NECESSARY
IF MAILED
IN THE
UNITED STATES

"Thought you might be wanting these two back," Wade said, nodding toward the horses. He wore frayed work jeans, a deep gray T-shirt and a light-colored Western hat. Nobody looked more like a working cowboy than Wade Porter, and Joel resented him for it, especially since he'd somehow managed to round up the horses and return them without a trailer. The guy probably rode one of them bareback, from what Joel could tell, and tethered the other one alongside.

Joel was really starting to dislike Wade Porter.

"Thanks," Joel said. "Don't know how they got out."

Wade grinned like he knew the answer to that one. When he spotted Callie, his eyes lit up. "That was you driving that rig, wasn't it?"

"Yes. Why?"

Joel watched Callie's face and sensed the anger bubbling up inside her as if she didn't need anyone criticizing her driving.

Wade turned to Joel. "Man, oh, man, that was some kinda driving! Whoo-hoo!" Wade walked past Joel and came over to Callie, who sat at the kitchen table. "Let me just say, my heart was in my throat when I saw you whip around that corner and head right for those two animals. I'd been following them on horseback and I thought for sure you were going to hit them, but you maneuvered that rig like you were driving a fine-tuned racecar. I don't think I've ever seen anything finer."

Joel stood beside the still-open door, unable to move, stunned by the revelation. He had a hard time digesting what Wade was saying.

"This woman can outdrive anyone I've ever seen. She

avoided a major accident with the skill of a professional. I tell ya, it was amazin'. You should be mighty thankful she was behind that wheel and not someone else. I'm assuming your daughter is fine?"

Joel nodded, powerless to speak.

"As soon as I saw you drive up, I went after your horses, not wanting them to cause any more near misses, or worse."

"Thank you, Wade," Polly told him.

"Now," Wade said to Joel, "let me show you how to fix that corral gate so those ornery animals can't escape again."

Joel simply nodded and followed Wade outside, still trying to assimilate everything he'd just learned. He felt certain now that if he'd been behind the wheel, things may not have gone, as well.

That one thought rattled him to his core.

# Chapter Seven

By the time Wade left, he'd fixed just about every latch on the ranch, and Joel couldn't have been more impressed by his knowledge and generosity. He finally realized that accepting help from someone was a good thing, especially when that someone knew what they were doing and was willing to teach him...which Wade had done. That was the secret—learning how to do it for himself, with the assistance of an expert, a live expert instead of a video.

Now Joel felt confident he could repair or replace any latch, lock, broken gate or doorknob anywhere. Not that any of them would need his newfound expertise since he'd officially accepted Wade's help and asked him to come by on a weekly basis. He was grateful and pleased that Wade had agreed.

Joel recognized how bullheaded he'd been, and it took a near accident to make him understand that people in the country liked to help out whenever they could. All he had to do was say yes...which he finally did to Wade, and whoever else Wade wanted to bring by. The fence still needed mending, and there were still a ton of jobs to do around the house and property, particularly that roof. He hadn't been back up there since he'd fallen off.

"I'll take that ride back to my truck now," Callie said as she entered the barn. Joel had just secured both Golden Girl and Rockabilly in their box stalls for the night and was about to walk over to the house to apologize to Callie for acting like a jerk.

"Sure," he said.

All at once, the sight of her took his breath away. She stood outlined by a full moon, her rich black hair tousled around her face, her pretty blue dress caressing her body like it had been tailored just for her curves, the color enhancing her deep blue eyes.

She wore one of his shirts draped over her shoulders, for warmth, no doubt. The night air had turned cold.

"I hope you don't mind, but the nights can get chilly around here and my jacket is back in my truck."

She slipped her arms through the shirtsleeves, then rubbed her forearms.

"Don't mind at all," he told her, loving how his shirt looked on her and wishing he could surround her with his warmth, that he could take her in his arms.

He didn't know if what he was feeling for her was due to the fact that she'd managed to avoid a horrible accident that afternoon or that he'd finally allowed all the pent-up emotions he felt for her to come pouring out. Either way, he wanted nothing more than to start all over again.

"I assume Polly took care of feeding you?" he asked.

"Yes, and I made a pig out of myself, two bowls of soup and three slices of bread with plenty of butter.

Polly's chicken noodle soup is the best. Just the way I remembered it from when I'd spend the entire day here with Sarah, helping out with chores."

"Sarah told me so little about that time. Anything I knew about it, I learned from you."

"I haven't really thought about any of that in years. Too angry, I suppose."

Golden Girl poked her head out of the boxed stall, blew out air and stomped a foot.

Callie went over to her and stroked her neck. The mare seemed to love it and nudged in closer.

"She likes you. I'm still a little awkward around them. I think they pick up on it. I was always envious of you and your family…from some of the stories you'd tell about living on the ranch, and your love of animals."

"In all that time we were together, I don't think you ever really told me much about your folks." Callie continued to stroke Golden Girl.

"That's because there wasn't anything much to tell. I grew up in private boarding schools mostly, and only came home for holidays and for a couple weeks during the summer. My parents were always too busy to have me around."

"That's too sad. I guess I was lucky. Still am. I live on the family ranch with my parents and one of my sisters, Kenzie, who more or less runs things now. My dad still makes the final decisions, but it's Kenzie who handles the day-to-day stuff.

"My mom does most of the cooking. Not that we all don't know how. We do. And some of us are good cooks, but there's nothing like Mom's. You, Polly and

Emma should come over this Sunday night for dinner. That's when my mom typically outdoes herself."

The invitation brightened Joel's spirits and made him hopeful for a budding friendship. "That would be nice. I know Polly would love it, and so would Emma."

"Then Sunday it is. Now, I really should be heading home."

Golden Girl whinnied when Callie stopped petting her.

"She doesn't want you to leave just yet," Joel urged, "and neither do I."

It was the first time they'd had a real conversation since he'd arrived in Briggs, and he didn't want it to end so soon.

A genuine smile flashed on Callie's face. "She's a real sweetheart."

Callie ignored his comment about wanting her to stay, so he let it go.

"I think she's glad to be home," Joel said, thankful the horses were safe and unharmed. "They both walked right into their stalls tonight without so much as a flinch."

Callie now stood only a few feet away from Joel. She was so close he could almost reach out and touch her, but he controlled his desire.

"They have a sense about them. It was a tough day, and I'm sure they're happy to be home."

"We all are. Thank you for keeping yourself and my girl safe this afternoon. I'll be forever grateful."

Callie smiled, and he wanted to drop to his knees right there. A mere thank-you didn't seem like enough. Not only was he grateful for his daughter's safety, but he now realized just how grateful he was for Callie's safety. He couldn't handle it if anything happened to either one of them.

"Not a problem. I was only doing what I'd been trained to do from years of driving a truck on my ranch."

He took a step closer, hoping she wouldn't move away. He felt drawn to her, as if he'd lost all power over his emotions.

"Maybe so, but according to Wade, you saved lives."

"Thanks, but these guys had a little something to do with it, as well. They ran off in the opposite direction." She scratched Golden Girl behind her right ear, then stroked her long neck. "Didn't you, girl? You're one smart sweetheart, aren't you?"

Golden Girl moved back a few steps, then bobbed her head as if she was agreeing with what Callie had said.

Both Joel and Callie laughed at Golden Girl's antics. It was then that he knew he had to tell her the truth, when her defenses were down.

"I never loved Sarah."

Callie blanched and stared at him, the laughter draining from her face. "Joel, do you really want to go into this now?"

"You deserve to know the truth."

"Fine, but that's not what she told me. She said you two had been in love for months."

"She lied."

"Then you must have fallen in love with her while you were married or why would you have stayed?"

"I stayed for Emma, but we had separate lives. After Emma was born, I suspected Sarah was cheating on me, so I confronted her. She admitted she had, asked my forgiveness and told me the cheating was over, but that was a lie. She went right on with her affairs. For a while I thought about having my own affairs, and even came close once or twice, more to get even with Sarah than anything else. In the end, I couldn't do it. Not when I knew Emma was waiting for me to come home every night. I stopped pretending and admitted the truth. We were good for a few months, until Sarah started lying again. I tried to get her to stop. Even went to couples counseling, but Sarah was…well, she was your best friend. You probably knew her better than I ever could. She hated being tied down, especially to me. I know she loved Emma, but Emma was never enough. She wanted more of everything—more money, more fun, more freedom—none of which I could provide."

"That's not what we talked about when we were kids," Callie told him, turning away. "Back then we both wanted a houseful of kids, a husband who we could love with all our hearts and who loved us back. Everything else, like personal careers or where we would live or how much money we would have was an afterthought to our main goals. I don't understand any of what you're telling me. And I have a hard time believing it."

"I have no reason to lie to you, Callie. That young girl you knew was not the woman I married. I don't think Sarah wanted even one child, let alone an entire houseful. Sarah was leaving me that day. Leaving me for another man. Apparently, that wasn't the first time she considered leaving me for another man. She told me she'd almost left me two other times, but stayed because of Emma. She said they weren't father material, but apparently this guy had proven himself to be a good dad with his own son, so she was leaving and taking Emma with her."

Callie wrapped her arms around her stomach. He could tell his words were having a physical effect on her. She turned back around to face him.

"I don't understand. What was she looking for?"

He shrugged. "I don't know. Love, I suppose. Or money. Maybe that's all she ever really wanted. We never talked about what was important. Our conversations were always kept on the surface."

"You make her out to be a shallow person. Why should I believe you?"

"Because deep in your heart, I think you always knew the real Sarah."

"Not like this. Does Polly know any of this?"

He could see tears pooling in Callie's eyes. He knew this had to be tough to listen to, but it was important for her to understand what had really gone on for the past six years.

"Yes...well, most of it anyway. She was there the morning before Sarah's flight when Sarah finally came clean. I'd suspected some of this, but couldn't be sure until that morning. Days before she left, she'd told me she was going to California to visit a girlfriend, but I accidentally came across a provocative message on her phone from another man. After that, Sarah confessed. She was leaving me, flying to Vegas with her lover on his private plane and taking Emma with her."

"That must have broken your heart."

"It did, and I begged her to reconsider taking

Emma, appealing to whatever motherly love she still felt for our daughter. I must have gotten through to her because at the last minute, she changed her mind about Emma and decided to leave her in Polly's care. Unfortunately, she didn't tell me she'd changed her mind, and left the house with Emma. When I first heard about the plane going down, I remember not being able to breathe or to think properly. I'd heard that all six passengers on that private plane were killed, including the flight crew."

Callie leaned back on a stall gate, all her defenses broken as tears moistened her face. He wanted to hold her in his arms, but he could tell by her stance that she wouldn't let him. "All those fun times we shared, all those dreams of happily-ever-after. Why? Why had she put herself on such a destructive path? What went on in your marriage or in her life that made her act out like that? Maybe I could have helped if I'd been more understanding, more forgiving and tried to talk to her."

Joel shook his head. "I'm sure there was nothing either one of us could have done. Even her therapist couldn't seem to help her."

"What about her mom? I thought she and her mom were close—at least, that's what she always told me."

He'd never considered that Callie didn't know about Sarah's mom. The fact that Sarah hadn't told Callie sent a chill down his back. He really hadn't known what went on with his wife at all.

"Callie, I assumed she told you…her mom abandoned her when she was seventeen. Told her she was old enough to make it on her own, gave her a hundred dollars, kissed her on the cheek and left with a man

Sarah hadn't ever met. Polly took her in and helped get her into college. Her mom would call Sarah once in a while asking for money. Sarah would always find a way to get it to her, either through Polly or, later, through me. Since Sarah died, we haven't heard from her. She's never even met Emma."

Callie shuddered. He didn't want to hurt her, but she had to know the truth, had to know what really happened.

"I don't understand why she didn't tell me about her mom."

"I only found out about it through Polly. Sarah didn't like to talk about her mom much. I think she somehow felt it was her fault that her mom left. That she'd done something to push her away. I tried to get her to open up countless times, but she never would."

Joel could tell that Callie was doing everything she could to hold back the emotion that racked her body. He hated what all this information was doing to her, and decided he'd said enough for one night.

She looked over at him—tears streaking her face, her forehead knotted, her eyes searching his for answers he didn't have. "There must have been something…"

Without thinking about it, Joel leaned in, took Callie in his arms and held her tight. She reached around him and slid into his warmth, crying on his shoulder, allowing him to soothe her. His own emotions were still raw and came crashing up, burning his eyes and his throat. They stood there for what seemed like a long time, finding comfort in each other. Trying to cope with the pain. When he felt Callie's body begin to relax, he gently brushed her lips with a kiss, tangling his fingers in her hair. The years they'd been apart didn't seem to matter. His emotions ran deep for Callie...always had.

He'd always pretended that he didn't love her anymore. That he'd gotten over her, but now he knew she was in his blood and there was nothing he could do to change it.

Holding Callie, he realized for the first time that Sarah must have known, must have realized he never stopped caring about Callie.

Joel pulled away from Callie as the revelation took hold of him, as it crept up his spine and tightened his throat.

"Maybe if I'd been honest with myself about how I'd felt about you, been able to tell Sarah the truth, things might have gone differently."

"We can't change the past, Joel. What you did, and what Sarah did, already happened. We can only move forward."

"Does that mean you'll give me another chance?"

She stared at him for what seemed like ages. Then she said, "I should go, Joel. Maybe Polly can drive me to my truck."

"Something happened to me that morning, Callie. I saw clearly what was important to me...what really mattered in my life, and how much family and place meant to me. I was scared to admit it when I was young, when you and I were together. I was scared because I thought I was my father's son and couldn't give myself to anyone. But when that plane went down and I thought my Emma was on it, my entire world came crashing down around me. I'd never in my life felt a hurt so deep or so profound. Words can't describe how I felt that morning. Then, when Polly called to tell me Emma hadn't been on that plane, that she was safe, with her, I knew what I had to do...how I had to change. I know now that I agreed to move to Briggs with Polly not simply because it was a place to go, but because you were here. Callie, I..."

"Joel, please stop."

She wiped the lingering tears away from her eyes.

"Callie, I'm sorry. I thought..."

"I need time, Joel. Time to absorb everything."

She looked deeply into his eyes as if she was searching for answers, anything that might help her to understand.

He reached out for her, but she stepped away.

"I can't do this... I'm not... I'm sorry, but I just can't."

Then she spun around and hustled out of the barn.

THE NIGHT HAD been long and restless as Callie's thoughts looped with everything that had happened and what Joel had told her about his life with Sarah. But what gave her nightmares was the thought that because of a last-minute decision on Sarah's part, little Emma was not on that doomed flight.

Callie felt as though she'd been run over by a double-decker bus. Her shoulders and upper arms ached from holding on to the steering wheel with a death grip, and when she removed the bandage from her cheek, a bright red line ran the length of her cheekbone.

"Pretty," she said to herself in the bathroom mirror.

The bruise on her chin had finally healed, but now she had the cut on her cheek to contend with.

Everyone in her family had been out when she arrived home last night, so there was no one to fuss over her injury or ask her questions. She truly hadn't been in the mood for an inquisition. Not that she could have kept it to herself, but her parents had enough going on with the ranch taking a financial hit last year due to the drought, and her sister Kenzie was working long, hard days to try to make the ranch profitable again. A night on the town probably did them all a world of good. She wished she'd been able to join them.

Instead, she'd been home, in bed early, licking her wounds, so to speak.

Now everyone in the house was still sleeping. Dawn hadn't even made an appearance yet over the Teton mountain range, so Callie decided to take a shower, get dressed and catch some R & R of her own.

With everything she'd learned and the way she'd felt wrapped up in Joel's arms, her emotions were a jumbled mess. All she knew was that she needed a morning of fishing to sort out her thoughts.

She felt differently toward Joel now, as if she was beginning to understand what he'd gone through, what he was still going through. For the first time since she'd met Joel, she felt actual empathy for him.

Never would she have guessed that word would ever apply to her feelings for Joel Darwood, yet there it was as clear as spring water in a shallow pond.

The hot shower seemed to strip Callie of all the aches and pains in her shoulders and arms, giving her the boost she needed. After enjoying the soothing shower for at least a full fifteen minutes—any longer and she'd feel guilty for wasting precious water—she toweled off and slipped on her favorite jeans and deep blue long-sleeved T-shirt over black undies. Then she grabbed her fishing gear from the corner of her room where she kept it, gingerly tiptoed down the stairs and through the house, plucking a sweater off a hook next to the front door as she walked out.

By the time she stepped outside, the sun was starting to rise. She hoped the ride and the beautiful view of the Tetons would help her to understand all that Joel had told her about Sarah's destructive behavior. The revelations about their life had been shocking. All those years Callie had assumed that Sarah and Joel had lived an idyllic life together. That Sarah had settled down, had found a purpose, and she and Joel were crazy in love with each other.

Now she knew she couldn't have been more wrong on every level, and regretted not reaching out to Sarah during that time…forgiving her…forgiving Joel.

As soon as Callie stepped into the stable, Miss Silver Pistol poked her head out of the stall, seemingly eager to get this day going.

"There's my girl," Callie said to Miss Silver Pistol, a paint she'd loved ever since the first moment her dad brought her home four years ago.

Within fifteen minutes, Callie was mounted and on her way down the narrow path that took them to the bend in the Snake River that meandered through the very tip of the Grant ranch, where she knew her brother, Carson, and their dad, Henry, were fishing, like they had done every Saturday morning since Carson was a boy.

She dismounted, tied Miss Sliver Pistol to a tree, shrugged on her fishing vest and pulled up her high rubber boots, seized her rod and reel and walked out to meet the men in the sparkling river. A cool whisper of a breeze danced over her face and played in her hair, reminding her of how much she loved these quiet moments out on the river.

"Well, I'll be," her dad, Henry, said, gazing over at her, his weathered face beaming. "Ain't seen you out here on a Saturday mornin' for weeks. Thought you finally gave it up."

Her dad, a tall, thin working cowboy with graying hair and a content disposition, wore his usual plaid shirt, string tie over an open collar and jeans. Both the shirt and jeans had pressed seams that her mom would spend hours making sure were exactly centered on each garment. Ironing day came once a week on Wednesdays and was never missed. Ritual was part of her mom's daily life, and she balked whenever she had to break her rhythm.

Gazing out at her dad, with his thick gray hair and trim physique, and Carson, the rough-and-tumble cowboy, who both rarely missed a Saturday fishing, except when Carson had been on the road or if the river froze, she suspected some of that habitual rhythm had rubbed off on them, as well.

"Just took a break is all," Callie told him. He nodded and went back to fly casting, the sun catching his line as he tossed it back and forth a few times, then released it into the air and gently landed it in the rippling water.

For a long while, none of them spoke. Instead, they each concentrated on their lines resting on top of the water. Callie could feel the tension of the previous night and day slowly drain from her body. There was nothing like a morning on the river to wash away her fears. It had always worked, even when she was a kid. There was something about being out in the sunshine, under a bright blue sky, watching sunlight dance over the meandering water and listening to the babble of the river as it ambled over rocks that calmed her soul.

She always felt at peace out on the river, and supposed that was the same reason why her dad and brother tried to get out every Saturday morning.

"Heard you nearly ran over some ponies yesterday afternoon," Carson said as he trudged through the water in her direction, breaking her trance. "And I see there's a nasty scratch on your face. Mom couldn't have seen that yet or it would be covered in bandages."

"She hasn't. I managed to sneak out before she got up."

He looked concerned, those dark eyes of his narrowed, and his forehead furrowed.

"Are you okay?"

"I'm fine, but how'd you hear about what happened?"

"Wade Porter and I shot some pool last night at Belly Up."

Callie realized once again that nothing got past her family. Their connections in the town spread far and wide.

"He told me about your driving skills. Always knew you were good, but from the way Wade told it, you should be driving for NASCAR."

"I did what I had to do."

Callie secured a new fly to the end of her line, did a few false casts, then flung her line as far out into the river as she could, a perfect shot.

"Wade told me about you and Joel, as well. I knew

he was living on the Double S Ranch, but I thought you would've stayed as far away from him as possible, what with everything that happened between you two."

Of all Callie's siblings, Carson was the one she could go to with problems. It was like that for all her sisters, as well. Always had been. He was the voice of reason. The brother who could be trusted with their deepest secrets, or at least that was how he always came across. More times than not, however, once Carson knew a secret, sooner or later the entire family knew. The good thing in all of it, he was the only one in the family who knew how to guide each of his sisters to make the right decision.

He'd told Callie years ago that it might be time to reach out to Sarah, but Callie would never listen to him. Her anger and hurt had run too deep.

Now she wished she'd listened.

"His daughter, Emma, is in my kindergarten class," Callie told him.

"I hear she's the spittin' image of her mom."

Callie hesitated before answering him, as if admitting Emma's resemblance to her mom somehow had any bearing on how Callie treated Emma…which it most certainly did not. "There's some resemblance, yes."

"Does that bother you?"

She turned to him, losing control of the line. "Of course not," she said a little too forcefully. Emma's resemblance to Sarah was almost surreal, down to the streak of white-blond hair that blended into her bangs, and slid down the right side of her head exactly as it had on Sarah. Her friend had hated the streak, and even as a teen she'd dye it to match her blond hair so kids wouldn't make fun of her.

"Why should it?" Callie said, suddenly feeling defensive.

"Oh, I don't know." He shrugged. "Maybe because Sarah was your best friend and she betrayed you. And seeing Emma every day only reminds you that you still haven't gotten past the hurt."

"Yes, I have. That was a long time ago. I'm *way* past that. Matter of fact, Joel and I are friends now."

"You don't say?"

"Yes, and who knows, it may progress into more." She hadn't meant to say that. It just came out.

Carson raised an eyebrow. "Are you sure you want to go down that road again?"

Callie's sudden confidence waned, and she wanted nothing more than to cry on her brother's shoulder. Her eyes watered, and she felt the hitch in her throat.

She and Carson took a few steps away from their dad.

"Oh, Carson. I don't know anything anymore. Everything I'd assumed about Joel and Sarah seems to be false. If what he told me yesterday is true, all my happily-ever-after scenarios I'd dreamed up for them were completely wrong. They weren't happy. They were miserable. Sarah had put herself on a self-destructive path almost from day one of their relationship. I'm not saying it was all her fault—Joel takes half the blame—but he told me he never loved her. All this time, I thought he had. It was all lies."

Carson put his fishing line down on a rock, pulled his sister in closer and gave her one of his bear hugs while she cried on his shoulder like she had many times before. The comfort of his strong arms and his soothing voice telling her it would be all right, allowed her to finally let go of the emotions she'd been holding inside ever since the near accident the previous day.

When she stopped crying and pulled away, she said, "I don't hate him anymore. Matter of fact, I think he's been through hell these last few years, and now he's really trying to make up for it. I just don't know if I can trust that he'll stay on this path. His past doesn't support that he will."

"As our dad always says, sometimes the past is best left where it is…"

Their dad, Carson and Callie all chimed in together, "In the past."

They all chuckled at once, Callie wiping her tears on her sleeve.

"Okay, so now what? What's your next step?" Carson asked.

Their parents had always taught them to tackle a problem head-on, and although it sometimes took each of them a while to figure out what that meant exactly, Callie now had a pretty good understanding what she should do.

"I invited Joel, Polly and Emma over for dinner tomorrow night. You're a good judge of character, when you're not blinded by emotion, so I was hoping you could sort of, well, maybe check him out. See if you think he's got some moral character going on, some backbone. That I'm not being sucked into his phony charms again."

Callie hoped Carson wouldn't be upset at her reference to her brother's being blinded by emotions—which directly related to Carson's relationship with

Marilyn Rose, a woman no one in the family had liked, but he'd gotten engaged to her before he came to his senses and fell for the love of his life, Zoe Smart. As a rule, the Grant siblings' were notorious at overlooking red flags in their relationships until it was too late to react properly.

"I'll be checking him out, as well, ya know," their dad said as he cast his line out into the flowing river, and as soon as he did, he snagged something hefty. Both Callie and Carson quickly trudged through the water to help.

"Reel it in, Dad," Callie yelled.

"It's a big one," Carson said as he grabbed a net to capture the beast. "I got it."

"Caught us Sunday dinner," their dad shouted, as Carson scooped up what had to be one of the biggest fish their dad had ever hooked. "Whoo-hoo! What a team we are! Ain't nothing that can get past us."

"Nothing," Callie said, hoping like heck that was true.

## Chapter Eight

Joel didn't know what to expect when he pulled his SUV in front of the Grants' ranch house early Sunday evening. Dusk threatened to settle in on the valley and the Grant house, with its redwood siding and tin roof that reflected the decreasing sunlight. Several other cars and trucks were already parked in a neat line along the front of the house and along one side. Joel had spotted a few more near what looked like stables only a few yards from the house. He could see people milling just inside the open front door and through the windows. The place looked more like there was a large party going on rather than a sedate Sunday dinner.

As soon as he turned off the engine, he could hear voices and laughter coming from inside the house. Apprehension raced through him. Joel had always felt awkward in these types of situations. Making small talk with strangers in a set environment had never been his forte, and he was especially apprehensive about meeting the rest of Callie's family.

What if they hated him? Then what?

"We might not be staying very long," Joel mumbled as he parked and turned off the ignition.

Polly turned to him, looking radiant. When she

worked on the ranch, tending to her horses, cleaning out stalls and running the house, she rarely wore makeup and lived in torn-up jeans, some kind of loose-fitting shirt and a ball cap. Tonight, she wore her blond hair down with a slight curl to the bottom, a tailored dark blue dress and flat dress shoes. Polly was an attractive woman who took pride in not only her ranch, but in her health and appearance, as well.

"You're letting your nerves get the best of you." Polly reached over and touched his arm. "The Grants are a warm and loving family. I've known Mildred and Henry for most of my life, and they would never do or say anything to make their guests feel uncomfortable. Callie would never have invited us if we weren't going to be welcomed with opened arms. Now tuck those nerves away and let's enjoy the evening."

Joel grabbed the round plastic container that held the carrot cake Polly had made, with Emma's help, and the bottle of red wine from the backseat. He stretched his neck from side to side to work out the tight muscles, then he headed for the house. Polly took the cake and started up the stairs, while Joel followed close behind.

Emma had already jumped out of the SUV and charged up the steps, excited about seeing Miss Callie. By the time she stepped on the covered wraparound porch, two golden Labs had come charging out the open front door, their bodies swinging with each wag of their tails. Emma stopped for a moment until Callie appeared in the doorway. "They won't bite, Emma. They only want to say hello."

"I don't like big dogs," Emma said, cowering away.

Callie tugged on each of the dog's collars, restraining them from getting too close to Emma.

"They live here, sweetheart, and they love children."

"I don't love them. They look mean, like they want to bite me."

"They might lick you, but would never bite you."

But Emma ran down the stairs to her dad. He scooped her up, and she instantly wrapped her arms around his neck. "I don't like those dogs, Daddy. They're too big."

"Tell you what, I'll keep the dogs tied up, Emma," Callie told her. "Once you go inside you won't even know they're here."

Then Callie walked the dogs to the far end of the porch and attached a leash to each one and secured them to the porch. The dogs immediately sat on their haunches as Callie fastened their leashes to the railing.

"What if they get away? What if they come in and bite me? What if they bite my dad or Auntie Polly? They could die. I could die. Everybody could die." Her little arm went up making a big air circle. "I don't want to be here. I want to go home. Now, Daddy. Take me home. I don't like Miss Callie or her mean ole dogs."

Callie took a couple steps forward, looking as though she was ready to say something to quell Emma's apprehensions, but Joel spoke up instead. "Look at me, Emma."

In the last few months, he'd had a lot of experience with trying to get his daughter to control her emotions before she worked herself up into a frenzy. He could only imagine that Callie had had to deal with it, as well, and hoped that didn't impact how she felt about

Emma. He knew his daughter could be a handful, but he trusted that Callie had the skills to handle her.

Emma reluctantly let go of his neck and obeyed her dad, as Callie petted the dogs sitting calmly by the porch railing. "See. Miss Callie tied the dogs up, just like she said. They aren't going anywhere. I promise. Now, I want you to take a deep breath and calm down. Okay?"

Emma gazed at the dogs, then back at her dad.

"Okay," she said in a soft voice.

Joel could tell she was calming down, could feel the release in her little body as she leaned against him.

"Are you better now?"

She nodded.

"I'm going to put you down, okay?"

She nodded again as Joel put her down on the step next to him.

"You should apologize to Miss Callie for wanting to go home, and for saying you don't like her when I know that's not true."

Emma rubbed her eyes with her fists, then took her dad's hand as he led her up the steps.

When they got onto the porch, Emma slid out of her father's grasp and stood a few feet away from Callie.

"I'm sorry," Emma whispered.

"I didn't hear you, Emma. You'll have to speak up," Callie said, using her teacher voice. Joel recognized that voice from hearing her use it in her classroom. It always sounded stern, but with a dash of kindness.

"I'm sorry," Emma repeated, sounding much more sincere.

"Thank you, Emma," Callie told her, bending down to her level, then giving her a hug. "I know that if you're not used to a big dog, it can be intimidating. I'm sorry if they scared you."

"It's okay, Miss Callie. They can't hurt me now. They're all tied up."

"Yes, they are."

"Should we go inside?" Polly said to Emma, taking her hand as Callie's mom came to the door to greet them. Within moments, Polly and Emma disappeared inside, leaving Joel on the porch with Callie.

"Sorry about that. Emma has a very active imagination, and sometimes it gets the better of her."

He blamed Emma's behavior on the fact that up until he'd moved to Briggs, Emma's home life had been chaotic, and once Sarah died, Emma sometimes spun the simplest of events into crazy tales.

"I know. I've had to deal with it during class," Callie answered.

He'd figured as much, but hoped it wasn't too bad.

"Is this something we need to officially talk about?"

Callie smiled. "Not yet. Plus, seeing how you handled her just now will help me in the future."

"Great. I really want this to work, Callie. She loves it here in Briggs, and so do I."

Just seeing Callie again, in her own element this time, made him want to kiss her and never let her go. He was still so very grateful for her quick thinking behind the wheel. Besides, he couldn't shake the memory of her warm response to his holding her in his arms.

"I'm glad, Joel. It's a great place to raise a child."

He liked her response, liked how she'd looked at him and smiled when she said it, as if she really meant it.

Things were looking up.

The only reason he'd agreed to this dinner was precisely because of that moment in the barn. He'd thought about backing out a couple times, but then always reconsidered. Even though she'd stopped him from kissing her, he could tell somewhere deep inside she still cared for him. He'd decided he could cope with the awkwardness of meeting her family if that was what it took to get back in her good graces again.

He had hoped to get some alone time with Callie, but from the sound of all the voices coming from inside the house, he no longer thought that was possible.

"Seems like you have a houseful," Joel told her as they stood next to each other. Glancing along the front porch, he noted the comfortable-looking chairs, rockers and a wooden swing that hung from the ceiling at the far end.

"We have about fifteen tonight," Callie answered, her face beaming. She wore tight-fitting jeans, tan cowgirl boots and a crisp wine-colored Western shirt open at the collar, revealing something pink and lacy underneath. He couldn't help the bedroom thoughts that meandered through his mind at the sight of all that lace.

Oh, yeah, he had it bad for her, and there was nothing he could do to change that.

"Dinner won't be ready for another half hour or maybe longer. Mom invited our cousin, Father Beau from St. Paul's Church, and he had a late baptism to perform. We're holding dinner until he gets here. I thought we could take a little ride first. Are you up for it?"

Joel wasn't too keen on riding yet. Polly had been trying to teach him, and he'd gone out once on his own, but so far, he didn't particularly like it. Mostly, he'd been nervous about getting up on a horse. Worried that he'd fall off, or the horse would run off and he wouldn't know how to stop it.

"Sure," he told her. The old Joel would lie about his abilities, but this new guy who wanted nothing more than to be the best man he could be decided to come clean. "To be honest, though, I'm not very good at it."

"Don't stress. My brother, Carson, will be joining us to give you a few pointers."

So much for being alone with Callie, he thought.

"Wait. Your brother? The bronc rider? The rodeo hero? He's going to give me a few pointers?"

Joel knew all about Carson. You couldn't live in Idaho without knowing about Carson Grant, even if you didn't really follow the rodeo circuit. Callie's brother was by far one of the best bronc riders in the history of bronc riders. The man was a legend, a hero, winner of every title he could win in his category. This man would be giving Joel pointers?

She nodded, smiling. "Yes. Don't be intimidated. He's a sweetheart. He's not going to give you a bucking horse, if that's what you're worried about. He teaches kids how to ride over at M & M Riding School. He and his wife, Zoe, have our more friendly horses saddled up and ready to go. Zoe is six months pregnant, and won't get on anything that goes faster than a steady walk. Carson, well, he might take you up to a canter."

Callie took his hand and led him out to the stables, which were only a few yards away from the house.

When they arrived, she pulled Joel inside, and with each step, he started thinking worst-case scenario—as if this was going to be her brother's way of getting even for all the pain Joel had inflicted on Callie back in college.

"Hey," Carson said as they approached him, a big, warm smile on his face. Joel recognized him from news articles he'd seen about Carson Grant over the years. He had to admit he felt honored to meet him.

"Carson, Zoe, this is Joel Darwood, and he's super excited to be getting a few riding tips from you, Carson."

"My sister is one of my biggest fans. I hope she hasn't put the fear of God in you. I'm not going to teach you how to buck off a horse, I promise."

Joel chuckled, relieved that her brother seemed like a stand-up guy and wouldn't do anything crazy to punish Joel for his past transgressions...at least not tonight. "That's a relief. But honestly, I've heard about you for a long time, and it's great to finally get to meet you."

Joel hoped that by telling Carson the truth, he might go easy on him.

Carson chuckled and stuck out his hand. The two men exchanged a firm handshake. "Thanks. Great to meet you, too, Joel."

Then he took Zoe's hand, but with a much less aggressive handshake.

"I'm sure you'll enjoy the ride, Joel," Zoe told him, a sweet smile on her pretty face. She had possibly the reddest hair he'd ever seen, and skin so white it looked like porcelain. They seemed like a good match: the rugged cowboy and the lady. Joel wondered how long they'd been together and if their love affair had had a rocky start? After all, a guy like Carson must be on the road for most of the year. That had to be tough on a relationship.

But then Joel realized he was merely comparing it to his own failed romance, competing in a sense, and he didn't want to be that guy anymore. No, he wanted what Carson had: a loving wife, a home, an extended family, a baby on the way and a thriving career.

Now all he had to do was figure out how to get it.

He turned to Callie. "I'm ready whenever you are."

"Then let's get this show on the road," Callie said, and they mounted up and headed out with Joel feeling a lot more confidant.


"Whoo-hoo!" Joel yelled for about the hundredth time, slapping his cowboy hat against his thigh as he and Callie made their way back to the house after the ride of his life. It was the first time he'd ever enjoyed riding a horse. Up until Carson had taught him how to handle a full gallop, he'd been afraid to move in the saddle, afraid that he was pulling on the reins too tight and afraid that he wouldn't be able to guide or stop a horse. "That was really terrific! I had no idea riding a horse could be that much fun."

He felt exhilarated and confident that he could eventually be a darn good horseman. All he had to do was sign up for a few more lessons at the riding school Carson had mentioned, and he'd have this thing nailed. He planned on signing Emma up, as well.

"You're a natural, Joel. When you relax, you have the balance and control of a true horseman, something that not everyone has." Callie walked alongside Joel as dusk settled on the land, giving everything a fiery orange glow. The Grant ranch was a thing of beauty with rolling hills, tall pine trees, and a clear view of the Teton mountain range.

"It helped that I was riding next to your brother. I felt almost impervious to falls or missteps. Besides, he said all the right things to get me to relax."

"Like what?"

"Like the horse wants to please me, and how I have to show him who's in control. I never thought of it like that before. Since Polly brought those two mares home, I've been trying to ride them with the..."

"...the help of an online video, no doubt."

He gently chuckled while he settled his hat back on his head. "No doubt. I'm learning that having a real live person teaching me things really makes a difference. Especially since I can ask a question and they'll respond."

"Funny how that works," Callie told him, smiling. His heart bounced in his chest. He hadn't felt this happy in months, possibly years.

"It's something I have to get used to. My parents weren't much on teaching me how to accept help, and whenever I went to them for assistance, they'd tell me I needed to figure it out on my own. I had to learn how to tough it out. Stand on my own two feet. It had the opposite effect on me. I felt insecure about almost everything."

She nodded in his direction. "That had to be tough. My parents are the exact opposite. Mom will get the pom-poms out whenever she even suspects one of her kids needs help with a subject, and my dad will gather all the information he can, sort it all out, present all the facts on the subject in a chronological order and even give you a history. Then there's each of my siblings, but I don't think we have enough time for me to list everything they want to do to help."

Joel wished he'd grown up with all of that, and only recently was trying to do some of that for his daughter.

"You're lucky to have them, Callie."

"I know. And what's even better is you get to meet them all in…well…now."

They'd walked back up on the front porch, and she was about to go through the open doorway when Joel took her hand in his and stopped her. Now that he'd brought up his folks, it might be the perfect time for a talk. He wanted to clarify a few more things.

"Can we take a few minutes, Callie? There's more I'd like to tell you. Why I reacted the way I did back in college. How I feel now."

He guided her off to the side of the front door for some privacy. She seemed willing to follow.

"Joel, I don't know if this is the right time. Everyone is waiting for us to come inside."

"We can't keep avoiding the elephant in the room." He looked around. "Or in this case, the elephant on the ranch." He took a step closer to her, and when she didn't back away or pull her hand from his grasp, he felt certain that she was ready to hear more of the truth about why he took up with Sarah when the only person he had cared about was Callie. "It might help you to understand."

"You and Sarah really hurt me, Joel. I almost dropped out of school because of it. You have to understand, that even now, this minute, I still have my doubts." Her eyes were moist. He hated that she suffered from his reckless behavior.

She didn't let go of his hand, but she took a step back.

"I know and I don't blame you, but please believe me when I…"

"Daddy! Daddy! We're sitting down to have dinner now." Emma bounded through the doorway, waking the two dogs who'd been sleeping. They both stood, as if waiting for Callie to release them from their shackles so they could play. "Auntie Polly told me to come get you, Daddy. And Miss Callie, too."

Emma reached out and grabbed Joel's free hand and pulled him toward the door. Much to Joel's regret, Callie instantly let go of his other hand, then walked over to soothe her dogs. He felt as though the rug had just been pulled out from under him. He was all set to spill everything, and Callie was finally willing to listen with an open heart.

"We better go in," she said, approaching Joel. "My mom will hold up dinner until everyone is seated. She likes to serve her meals piping hot."

"Couldn't we just skip…"

But Callie wouldn't listen, and instead walked right past him and disappeared inside.

"Come on, Daddy. You don't want to miss dinner. Mrs. Grant made chicken and dumplings, corn on the cob and mashed potatoes and, well, all sorts of stuff. She even has a homemade cherry pie and a blueberry pie to go with our carrot cake for dessert. And apple fritters. They're my favorite."

"Since when?"

"Since I got to help make them." Emma pulled harder on his hand. "Come on, Daddy. You don't want to miss the apple fritters, do you?"

"Not the apple fritters. They're my favorite!"

"Oh, Daddy!" Emma giggled, then they walked inside.

CALLIE HAD WANTED to linger out on the porch for a few more minutes and hear Joel out, but Emma had taken center stage. Even during class, Emma tried her best to pull all the attention to herself, so much so that Callie had to sometimes take a firm tone with her.

Heaven help her, but Emma was sometimes a challenge so forceful that it took everything she'd learned about tolerance and calm behavior around children not to lash out with a terse word or comment she would later regret.

She didn't know how Polly and Joel could be around her 24/7 and not give her a time-out every other minute.

Callie rotated her tight shoulders and released her clenched jaw as she took her seat next to Joel at the dinner table. Fortunately, Polly sat on Emma's left side, and Polly seemed to have more control over Emma than her dad.

Callie was anxious to get Carson's opinion of Joel. With some fifteen or so people around the dinner table, that wasn't going to happen anytime soon.

The entire Grant clan had shown up for dinner. Coco—who'd brought along Punky, whom Emma seemed to like just fine despite his somewhat reluctant behavior to warm up to her—had helped their mom in the kitchen with a last-minute dinner crisis. She sat at the far end of the table, near their mom, with Punky curled up in Coco's lap.

Kenzie, who still looked a little dusty from both working the ranch all day and stalling the horses for the night, poured the water and opened the bottles of wine.

Father Beau, wearing his black cassock, sat next to Callie's youngest sister, Kayla, while her husband, Jimmy, sat right next to her. Their toddler son, Hunter, slept in a stroller, draped with a thin blue blanket— he'd eaten earlier and was now down for the count. Carson and Zoe took the two empty seats directly across from Joel and Callie. Her dad and mom sat at either end of the massive table.

The unexpected guest was Miss Sargent, who Callie had replaced at school. She sat next to Polly. The two women seemed to not only know each other, but from the way they were chatting, Callie got the impression the two women were still good friends.

All the food on the table smelled delicious. Even the okra, Callie's least favorite veggie, smelled delectable. Callie never took to cooking. Sure she knew how, living in this house—even Carson knew how to make a standing rib roast—but she never took to it like Coco, had who found it therapeutic. Callie just found it to be a nuisance.

"Is it always like this on Sunday night?" Joel asked as he placed a white napkin across his thigh.

"Every Sunday. Mom doesn't like anyone she knows to be alone on Sunday night. There've been some dinners where we've had to bring in extra tables from the barn. There was even a night when the town experienced some flooding, and our house and barn became a shelter. She says it's her way of giving back to the community that's been so good to our family."

"How so?"

"When my dad had his accident on his tractor and nearly lost the use of his right hand, our neighbors along with most of the shopkeepers took up a collection so he could go to a specialist at UCLA. That doctor saved his crushed hand. And when my mom fell and broke her hip when we were kids, our neighbors pitched in to bring us meals for weeks while she was recovering. Then there's the town's phenomenal support for Carson. Once he started winning, most everybody contributed and bought him the best bronc saddle money could buy. My parents never quite got over that one. Sunday dinner is just one way they give back. There's so much more they both do, but we'd be here all night if I had to list everything."

"Your parents are very special people." She could see the sincerity on his face. "My parents are nothing like yours. I barely saw them when I was growing up, and Emma hardly knows them. They're always too busy working."

Callie couldn't imagine what she would do without her family around her. They meant everything to her.

"I remember you telling me something about them when we were in college. I'm really sorry, Joel."

"It is what it is. At least Emma and I have Polly. She's a jewel."

"Always has been. And, I can't forget my siblings. They're the best, but I would never tell them that." As she said it, she turned toward Carson so he could hear what she was saying.

"You're just trying to butter me up so I'll agree to

give a talk to your class," Carson teased. He wore his emotions clearly on his face. If he hadn't wanted to give the talk, he'd be dead serious right about now, but a smirk always told her he was on her side.

"You know how much they would love it."

"Fine," he agreed. "But we'll have to go over my schedule first."

"Any time you're available. Whenever you're free," Callie told him. "You're such a great brother. There isn't a sister on this planet who has a better brother."

Carson raised an eyebrow. "If only that were true." He turned to Joel. "Do you have any sisters, Joel?"

"I'm an only child."

"What a concept," Carson said. "My life would be so much easier."

"And dull," his wife told him.

Callie picked up a dinner roll and tossed it at him. He caught it in his right hand. "Thanks, sis!"

Father Beau leaned over the table and glared at them. "Do I have to tell your parents on you guys?" he goaded.

"No," both Callie and Carson said in unison, as Carson took a bite of his dinner roll.

"Then put down the bread and let's give thanks." Whenever Beau showed up for dinner, he usually said grace.

"I'll say it tonight, if that's okay?" Carson interrupted, still wearing that smirk. Callie wondered what this was all about.

"Fine with me," Father Beau said.

Carson hadn't said grace in months, and he never took the honors away from Father Beau. Callie instinctively knew something was up.

Everyone bowed their heads, even Emma, who seemed to know exactly what to do. Somehow Callie didn't think it was Joel who had taught her about praying before a meal, though he looked as though he was familiar with the practice.

"Thank you, Lord, for this food, for this family and for our friends, including a few new friends, Joel, Emma and Miss Polly, who are a blessed addition to this fine Sunday meal. Amen."

And in that instant, Callie knew Carson had told her everything she needed to know about how he felt about Joel. The thing was, Callie had already begun to trust him. That arrogance he'd carried with him to Briggs seemed to be waning.

Now all she had to do was learn how to accept Emma's peccadilloes, and she and Joel might actually have a chance.

# Chapter Nine

Joel had spent most of his night thinking about Callie, how she looked, how soft her skin had felt, her perfume, the fact that she'd taken the time to ask her brother to teach him to ride and how sweet she'd been to Emma. He knew his daughter could be challenging, but Callie seemed to know exactly what to say and do to avoid any problems.

Emma took after her mom, a free spirit. He had admired that in Sarah, probably why he'd been somewhat attracted to her in the first place. Unfortunately, Sarah didn't have any limits to guide her. She'd taken that sense of freedom, that rebellious ego, and turned it on the people who cared about her. He'd learned even her aunt Polly had experienced Sarah's hurtful ways when she wouldn't show up for a dinner they'd planned or a concert. Sarah would always have an excuse, Polly had shared with him, but it usually came the day after Polly had been stood up in favor of another person or event that Sarah had deemed more important.

Since he'd become a single parent, the most important thing Joel had decided to teach Emma was compassion for others, patience with people who cared about her, kindness toward friends and family, all traits that Sarah never seemed to grasp.

Her daughter seemed to be having the same trouble.

"But Daddy, Frankie likes to let me have his training time with Wheezy and Squeezy. He said so."

Joel had pulled up to the curb in front of Emma's school and was just about to get out of the SUV when Emma admitted that she took all of Frankie's training with the bunnies. Twice a week, the kids would set up a small track to teach the bunnies how to jump over the various hurdles, and lately, Emma got to train twice each time. Joel turned off the engine. Kids ran by, eager to get to their classrooms, as parents either escorted the younger ones inside or sat in their cars and trucks watching to make sure their children went inside the door.

"He may have said so, but I'm sure Frankie would like to take the bunnies through the hurdles himself sometimes. At least you should offer."

Joel got out, went around to Emma's side and helped her down. Aunt Polly had packed a scrambled-egg-and-cheese sandwich, Emma's favorite, a tangerine and a cheese stick along with a small milk. All foods Emma agreed to eat. She carried her lunch inside her yellow backpack. Emma's curly blond hair had been clipped back with a blue bow that matched her blue tights under her long white sweater. She looked adorable, all courtesy of Aunt Polly's morning patience. Emma hated to get up early and get dressed for school. Despite her continual protests and delays, somehow Polly always had her ready on time.

"We're not going inside until you promise to let Frankie train the bunnies when it's his turn today."

She looked up at him with that cherub face and those pensive eyes. "But Daddy, we'll be late and I won't get a good spot on the rug."

"I don't care. This is important. Promise me."

She tsk-tsked, stuck a fist on her hip and said, "Okay. I promise, but if he doesn't want to, there's nothing else I can do." Then she shrugged.

"At least you tried, and that's what matters."

She grinned and ran off toward the front door with Joel following along behind her. He wanted to catch Callie this morning before class started, and he only had a few minutes before the bell rang, so he hustled.

He'd never found another chance to be alone with Callie after Sunday dinner the previous night and had decided what they needed was a real date. No siblings, no kids, aunts or friends, just the two of them on a date, getting to know each other all over again. Not that he was at all sure she'd go. He only knew he had to ask her.

When he arrived at her classroom, ready to pop the question, Callie and all the students were huddled around the back door. Callie's sister Coco was examining one of the rabbit on a small table next to the hutch. Her stethoscope dangled around her neck, and she wore a serious look on her face.

Callie spotted him and walked right over.

"What's wrong?" Joel asked as she approached, hoping Coco had been rooked into giving a talk much like Carson had, and there was nothing really wrong with one of the bunnies. Emma would be devastated if something happened to one of those rabbit.

"Little Wheezy's been lethargic the last few days. Bunnies like to hide their misery, so I thought I'd ask my sister to come in and give the little guy a physical just to make sure he's okay. She thinks he has a cold, but she'll take some blood and run a few tests to make sure."

"I hope the little guy's all right. I'm sure the kids would be upset if it's maybe more serious. Especially Emma. He's all she ever talks about."

"He'll be fine. I'm sure it's nothing." She smiled and Joel's mood brightened. "I hope my family didn't scare you off last night. Sunday dinners at the Grant house can be intimidating."

"Not at all. I thought they were great, and I was wondering if you'd like to do it again sometime… dinner. I mean dinner, alone…not alone…with me." He took a breath, let it out and crossed his arms over his chest. "Would you like to have dinner with me tonight? Or maybe we could catch a movie? Or we could stop in at Belly Up for a drink? Whatever you want."

Her forehead furrowed. Not a good sign. "I think…"

The bell rang, cutting her off. All the kids came running inside, taking their places on the blue rug. Joel had no choice but to move out of the way and head for the door as she gathered all her little chicks in a circle.

He turned back around before he exited the classroom to see if maybe, by some miracle, she was looking his way.

Not only was she looking his way, but she wore a big smile, nodded and motioned for him to call her.

A powerful swell of joy engulfed him as a grin slowly stretched across his lips, then he turned and walked out of the room feeling triumphant.

As IT TURNED OUT, Polly had come down with a cold, so for their first date, instead of a late-night dinner in a cozy restaurant where Joel and Callie could talk, they stopped in at Pia's Pizza Parlor, which was always busy with kids, parents and deafening video games. The noise factor alone prohibited them from merely talking and getting to know each other again.

"I think we're going to have to put off any conversation for another time," Callie had shouted across the table as they shared a cheese pizza.

Joel grinned, nodded. "Are you free next Friday night?"

Callie bobbed her head as she folded the slice in half and took a big bite. Emma had already gone off to play with a few other kids from school, and Joel was anxious to get up and supervise. He didn't like to let Emma wander too far from his sight, and before Callie could finish her first slice, Joel had disappeared into the swarm of kids, leaving her to speculate if they would ever get time alone again.

For their next date they caught a movie, a kids' movie complete with singing dragons and talking bears. Emma had begged her dad to come along, and Joel hadn't been able to say no.

"Can we see it again, Daddy?" Emma had asked as Callie and Joel each held one of her hands and picked her up every few feet, swinging her in the air. Emma loved it.

"Maybe," Joel told her.

"Can we see it now?"

"I think it's time to go home now."

"But I want to see it again. Please, oh, please,

Daddy. I don't even need popcorn or a drink this time."

Apparently the movie was very popular. Reluctantly, Callie mentioned that it was running in three of the six theaters.

"I think we can catch the second half in theater four," Callie said, wanting to avoid Emma's alligator tears. Joel agreed to slip into the next theater and for the next two hours they watched parts of the dragon movie over and over again.

For their third try at dating, Callie set up a "real" dinner date. Polly had agreed to take Emma to the library for a book signing and reading by a local children's author. Callie had bought a new cocktail dress for the event, which was billed as a quiet dinner for two at Hot Tomato. She even stepped into a pair of black heels for the occasion and wore her hair up, with long, dangling earrings.

At the last minute, a potential boarder for two young mares wanted a tour of the stables, and Polly didn't want to pass up the opportunity. Joel couldn't disappoint his daughter, and Callie didn't want him to, so off the little trio went to the book signing where Emma had to have three different books signed, and a picture taken with the author. Afterward, Emma didn't want to go home. Instead it was burgers and shakes at Moo's Creamery, with the life-size plaster cow greeting them at the front door that Emma had to sit on for at least fifteen minutes. Needless to say, by the time Joel in his gray suit and Callie in her black cocktail dress were seated, the entire place buzzed about the best-dressed couple who had ever dined at

Moo's. Even the owner had to take a picture to hang on the wall.

The strange thing with all of these threesome dates stacking up, and it looking as if they were going to be the norm rather than the exception, Callie couldn't seem to say no whenever Joel asked her out. Even though she had to share him with a sometimes ornery Emma, she truly enjoyed being with him, which explained why she was now standing in front of a monster blue-and-red inflated jumpy room watching mostly her students, as they celebrated Wade Porter's four-year-old nephew's birthday on the Double S Ranch.

"This is so much fun," Emma told her as she peeled off her shoes and socks in order to crawl inside the massive bouncy room. "My daddy is the best daddy in the whole world."

"He sure is," Callie had to agree. Not only had Joel been the doting and attentive father, but he was slowly turning himself into a cowboy in the truest sense of the word. This party was a testament to his recently acquired neighborliness and his willingness to help someone out whenever he could.

Emma stopped before she slid inside. "Aren't you coming in, Miss Callie?"

The last thing Callie wanted to do was fall on her face with her students watching her. "Maybe later, Emma. You go on ahead and have fun."

Callie knew if she crawled inside that room with Emma that eventually Emma would do or say something that Callie would have to react to, and it probably wouldn't be too pleasant. Callie had acquired a lot of patience when dealing with Emma during the past couple weeks of threesome dates, but she didn't want to press her luck.

Emma crawled inside and joined the other squealing children as they jumped and tried to stay out of each other's way. Joel sat in the corner, supervising as best he could, and from what Callie could see, he was doing a darn good job of it.

He played a version of Simon Says, only it was Joel Says, and all the kids played along, laughing and giggling when he yelled, "Stop." There weren't any winners or losers, just a lot of silly fun.

Joel reminded her of her own dad sitting in the corner, laughing right along with the children. She had so many fond memories of her dad gathering all her siblings together, their cousins and friends out on the back lawn of the ranch, playing the same game. Of course, there wasn't a bouncy house then. Everyone jumped and rolled on the grass. Sometimes they'd play the water balloon toss game. That had always been Callie's favorite, specifically when she could toss the balloon to Carson and it would explode in his hands. She'd squeal with laughter when the balloon would drench his shoes and pants. Much like Emma was squealing with laughter every time her dad yelled, "Stop," and she'd fall into someone and knock them down.

Joel would ask her not to do that, but each time she'd repeat the same behavior, almost as if she were challenging him. Emma needed to learn to respect Joel, but it seemed as though he wasn't willing to take the necessary steps. Instead, he'd try to appease her, and Callie did the same when they were together.

It just seemed easier.

Callie headed back to the group of adults sitting and standing under the white canopy. She grabbed a root beer out of a cooler, popped off the cap, took a long cool drink, then sat on one of the folding chairs directly in the sun. Everyone else gathered in the shade, but Callie delighted in the heat of pure sunshine.

It was a cool, crisp October afternoon. The sun made everything sparkle with its golden warmth. It was a perfect day for an outdoor birthday party. Callie wore a light sweater over her gray Western shirt, and loose-fitting jeans and her favorite cowgirl boots. She thought the land would be more parched than it was and had anticipated a lot of dust, but the Double S was slowly making a comeback. Despite the fact that fall had arrived, more grass grew out of the once-dry earth than she'd ever seen before. It was almost as though the land itself was happy to be part of a family again.

"Aren't you coming inside the bouncy house?" Joel asked as he approached, holding a longneck bottle of beer. Callie loved to watch him walk. His swagger had always caused her to go weak in the knees, and today was no exception. There was something about the sway of his hips, the way his shoulders turned slightly with each step, and the self-assured look on his face. Her thoughts drifted to when they were first in love, how his mouth had felt on hers, on her skin, on her breasts. The way he'd looked at her when they made love, the scent of his skin when he was lying on top of her, when he was...

"I think I'll pass on the opportunity," she replied, cutting off her memories.

Emma yelled for her daddy to watch as she jumped

and twirled. He spun around to watch her for a moment. "You're the best," he yelled. Emma giggled and kept jumping. "She really seems to be adjusting to this place. It's been somewhat of a miracle. I was concerned when we first moved, but it's turned out good for all three of us."

He took the seat next to Callie, facing the bouncy room.

Emma yelled for him to watch her again. She did the same thing and Joel clapped. "That's really good, kitten."

He turned to Callie. "Let's find a quiet place to talk while Emma's occupied."

"I don't know if she'll let you go." Callie felt certain Emma wanted all of his attention.

"She'll be fine if I disappear for a bit. Wade's inside monitoring and she loves Wade. Let's walk on over to the porch. I think we can get some privacy there."

Emma seemed okay with his leaving, she was too busy tormenting one of the kids to pay much more attention to her dad. Callie decided now was as good a time as any to have that conversation with Joel that they'd been trying to have ever since Sunday dinner.

When they were finally off walking by themselves, away from the many guests who milled around tossing horseshoes or playing badminton or any number of games that were scattered on the front lawn, the back of Callie's neck suddenly felt tight.

"It's a great party," she said, trying her best to start the conversation with small talk in order to take a few minutes to relax.

"Yeah, glad to do it for Wade. He's been such a

help to us. I can't thank him enough. But Wade isn't what we need to talk about."

Callie's stomach clenched as he guided her to the side porch, instead of the front, where no one could see them. As soon as they stopped walking he took her in his arms and kissed her, a hard, passionate kiss that sent a shiver through her body. She couldn't help herself. She fell into him and went along for the tantalizing ride. His kiss was everything she remembered it to be, and then some. Her body ached for more when he abruptly pulled away.

"I've been wanting to do that every time we've gone out," he said in a whisper.

"Was it worth the wait?" she teased, then she kissed him again, with the same amount of passion as before, melting into him, allowing herself to drift into her desire for him, despite her apprehensions of losing her heart.

Again he pulled away. "Sure, but I don't want to wait anymore, and from that kiss, I'm thinking you don't, either. There's only one thing standing in our way, and we both know what that is…our past. We have to come to terms." He ran his thumb over her now puffy lips. "I've always loved how your mouth looks after I kiss you, all pink and swollen."

"No one has ever kissed me like you do, Joel. I can't help but react to it. That doesn't change anything. I'm still not comfortable with the desire I feel whenever we're together."

"Don't be," he told her, then he kissed her again. This time it was longer, and as their tongues touched she felt as if he wanted to consume her. She would let him if she didn't know what it might lead to.

Complete heartache.

Now she was the one who pulled away, walked to the front of the porch, and perched herself on the swing. He sat down next to her, slipping an arm over the back of the swing to get a better look at her. Her lips still tingled as his gaze rested on her mouth.

She desperately wanted more of him. Wanted to forget about their past and pretend it never happened, but she knew that wasn't possible.

"What do you want to say, Joel?" She folded her hands on her lap and looked him in the eye waiting for an explanation.

"I didn't mean to hurt you. Neither one of us had planned to hurt you. We were drunk, very drunk, so drunk that I barely remembered kissing her when we woke up the next morning. I didn't even remember walking her over to her dorm room. The entire night is still a blur. What I do remember is our argument, how I felt when I woke up in bed next to Sarah. Ashamed. Completely and totally ashamed. So much so that I couldn't think of facing you."

"Is that why you avoided me for the next six weeks? Why my best friend met me for lunch and told me that the two of you were together now, and I had to deal with it? You sent Sarah to do your dirty work? I expected more from you, Joel. You broke my heart."

"I was a coward and I'm sorry. I was afraid to face you. Afraid that I wouldn't find the right words, so instead I avoided the whole thing, and I'm truly sorry."

"I wasn't expecting a ring and a date, just a conversation about what we each expected in a mate and in a marriage. It wasn't supposed to turn into an argument, just a discussion. When you left, I thought for sure you'd cool off and come back so we could talk it over. But when you didn't, I tried to call you, but you didn't answer.

"Then when Sarah laid down the law and told me how you always had a thing for her, and that you loved her but were too afraid to break up with me, I felt as if my whole world had blown up into a million pieces. She said some hurtful things that day. Things I wanted to talk to you about, but I could never pin you down."

Joel slipped his arm from her shoulders. "I had no idea she said that. I never told her I loved her or that she and I were a couple. Heck, we hardly saw each other for those six long weeks until she told me she was pregnant."

Callie was beginning to understand everything now, beginning to see how her best friend had lied to her about the one thing that Sarah knew meant everything to Callie—a baby.

"So you're saying every time I saw you two together, that wasn't real?"

"Never. She would beg me for favors or claim she needed something and I was the only person who could provide it. After a while, I felt sorry for her so I'd do whatever she wanted because truthfully, no one else would. She told me you had abandoned her, and that you hated me and wanted to talk to me just to say hurtful things. She warned me to stay away from you. I only slept with her that one time. That's why, in the beginning, it was hard for me to believe it was my baby, but we did a DNA test, so I knew unequivocally the baby was mine."

Callie wrapped her arms around her stomach. She couldn't accept that Sarah had been so cruel when

Callie would have done anything for her. He had no reason to lie, but it was still hard for her to accept that her best friend had been that malicious. "You're going to sit there with a straight face and tell me that my best friend spread complete lies about me, and about you, and that you only slept with her once? Everyone in our circle said you two had practically moved in together."

"Those were her lies that she spread. Sarah liked to exaggerate everything. You know that. You know how she was."

Callie stood and walked to the railing, trying her best to digest all this information about a girl she'd once thought of as closer to her than her own sisters. "Then why did you marry her?"

Joel came over to her at the railing. They stood only inches apart, her heart thundering inside her chest as she stared into his eyes, trying to understand all of this.

"Because it was the right thing to do, Callie. I didn't know if we stood a chance, but we both agreed to try. For a while, I thought we might make it, might be happy, but as you know, it didn't last very long."

Her heart was breaking all over again for the friend she apparently never had.

He took her hand in his, gently caressing her fingers, causing a combustible heat to surge through her. Maybe she knew too much now. After all these years of wanting to know the truth, maybe not knowing the truth had been better. Her heart felt heavy with sorrow.

She leaned in closer and could feel his breath on her face. "Joel, I…"

"There you two are," Polly said as she walked up

onto the porch. "Everybody's waiting for you to cut the cake. Emma wants her dad to be there. You know how she gets when you're not around."

"I'll be right there," Joel told her without taking his eyes off of Callie.

"We should go," Callie told him, breaking the spell and turning toward Polly. "Thanks for coming to get us, Polly."

"I didn't mean to intrude," Polly whispered, once she and Callie were on their way back to the covered seating area. Joel tagged along behind them.

Callie slipped her arm around Polly's waist, and Polly did the same to Callie. "Your timing was perfect," Callie told her in a hushed voice. "We were just talking."

"It looked like more than talking. Are you sure I didn't interrupt something important?"

"Yes, as a matter of fact, you did," Callie told her, smiling, suddenly remembering the one event she loved like none other. "I was just about to invite you, Emma and Joel to the annual Briggs Whopping Fish Tale Contest next Saturday. I'm sure you remember the annual fish fry? Seems to me it was your husband who got the whole thing started in the first place."

"I'd forgotten all about it. Yes, he did, sometime in the late seventies, as I recall. We'd love to come," Polly agreed. "There's only one thing."

"What's that?"

Polly grinned and whispered, "I don't think Joel knows the first thing about fishing."

"Then, just like everything else in his life, he'll have to learn," Callie said, and the two women chuckled as they hurried to join in on the birthday fun.

## Chapter Ten

Wade had the patience of a saint. At least that was Joel's assessment as Wade tried for what seemed like the hundredth time to demonstrate how to properly cast a fishing line into the meandering river. They'd been practicing for hours and Joel still couldn't seem to get the hang of it. He really didn't want to look like a complete fool at the annual town event, so he needed to get this. Unfortunately so far, he didn't seem to have the aptitude for it.

*It's not like it's rocket science*, Joel thought as he studied Wade's stance, the location of his hand on the cork part of the rod and how his shoulders moved.

It sounded more like instructions for a good golf swing or how to hit a baseball farther than first base... neither of which Joel could do. He just wasn't good at sports—any kind of sports, and apparently fly-fishing was high on that list.

"You have to relax, Joel. You're too uptight. Just let it flow. Be one with the fishing rod, one with nature."

"Easy for you to say. You've been doing this since... what...you were five?"

"Three, actually. My grandma taught me. She loved to go fishing early in the morning, while everyone slept. She'd slip out and spend an hour or so at sunrise every Sunday morning. Usually caught that night's dinner. I always woke up at the crack of dawn when I was a kid, and since she lived with us after my grandfather passed, she'd take me out with her in order to give my parents a break. I have some excellent memories out on this river with my grandma. We fished nearly every Sunday morning until she passed when I was sixteen. She never liked to miss fishing on Sunday morning. I believe she would rather have missed Sunday services than Sunday fishing."

"What is it about the people in this town? Did everyone have a great childhood?"

Wade chuckled. "Some small towns are like that. Some others, not so much. We happen to be lucky here in Briggs. Good, solid stock. People who care about family, friends and community. That's not to say we don't have our share of troublemakers and ruffians, but for the most part, people here want to do what's best. Like teaching a greenhorn cowboy how to cast a line. You want to try it again?"

Joel took the rod and reel. "A greenhorn cowboy, huh? We'll just see about that."

Joel looked down at his fishing rod, and this time he scrutinized Wade's stance, the length of his slack line and how he eased the line out over the water before the fly landed. He focused on the false cast, the backward movement, then the forward cast, making sure he did each one in a straight line while holding the rod in his right hand, thumb on top of the cork grip, facing forward. No wrist action. He could only use his forearm with an equal amount of momentum on the back and forward action.

"Abrupt sharp stops at either end," Wade cautioned, demonstrating his instructions. "Always keep the false casts short, only allowing the line to fly on the forward stop, not the backward."

Once Joel focused, miraculously, the bright orange fly landed exactly in front of him, far out in the water where he allowed it to float.

"Hot damn, Joel, I think that was near about perfect. You really do catch on quickly."

"Not normally, but for some reason, lately, when I concentrate, I've been doing all right."

"It's because you've found your place, your niche in this world. My wife was a lot like that. Claimed she couldn't boil water until she picked her own corn from our garden and made up some of the best corn chowder I ever tasted. Claimed she couldn't jump a horse until she started riding Mountain Midnight, a sweet mare she bought over in Cody. And don't even get me started on how she thought she couldn't mend a fence until I caught her driving a backhoe, then digging the proper sized holes for the poles. The woman was a marvel."

Wade cast his line into the water, a beautiful graceful movement of simplicity in motion.

"I didn't know you were married, Wade. You never mentioned it."

"It's not something I like to dwell on."

Joel could only assume it was a nasty divorce, something Joel had thought about on countless occasions. He knew if he'd ever tried to divorce Sarah, she would have made his life a living nightmare, along with taking Emma from him. He'd had friends who'd divorced with kids and nothing ever seemed to go right.

"Sorry I brought it up. I know how contentious a divorce can get. Had a good friend go through one a few years back and it nearly broke him."

Wade pulled his line back in and beautifully cast it out again, the line rolling into the water without even a hint of a splash. "It wasn't a divorce. I would've thought Polly told you. My Megan passed away from complications due to lupus. She was only twenty-six years old. Pneumonia came out of nowhere and took her before we had a chance to fight it. No one should have to suffer like that."

Polly had never mentioned this to Joel. He felt like a fool for bringing up such an obviously devastating time in Wade's life.

"I'm sorry, man. I had no idea."

"It's okay. I've learned how to cope. It'll be three years this coming December. Takes a while to come to terms with something like that. We thought because she was young and we did everything the doctors recommended she'd get through it. Statistics were in her favor, but those drugs wore her down and complications set in. It was like the first thing went wrong, then the second thing, and pretty soon everything was going wrong, like dominoes, ya know?"

Joel could relate that domino effect back to his own life with Sarah.

"I get that. Once things start going bad, it's almost impossible to fix."

"Tell me about it. Sorry you lost your wife the way you did. That has to be tough. Plus, the loss is still fresh. You seem to be coping well."

"Have to for Emma's sake."

Joel didn't want to go into the details of his marriage, at least not now. Sarah's death had hit him harder than he'd thought possible. Sure they didn't have a marriage during those last two years, but there had been times in the beginning when he thought it might work out between them. When he and Sarah shared some great moments, particularly when Emma was born. He'd never seen Sarah so happy…genuinely happy. She always said Emma was the best thing they'd ever done. And Joel had to agree. Even now, when he would watch Emma sleep, he knew nothing he could ever do in his life would equal the euphoria he had felt when she was born. Emma meant everything to him, and because of her, he knew he could never resent or dislike Sarah again.

She had given him the best part of his life.

"Children are a gift," Wade said without looking Joel's way. "Megan and I were planning on at least three kids. She would've loved your Emma, cute and full of moxie."

"She tugs on my patience at times, but you're right. She's the one thing I did right in my life. I wouldn't change that for anything."

It was the first time Joel realized that despite everything that had happened between himself, Callie and Sarah, he wouldn't go back and change one darn thing if it meant he wouldn't have Emma with him.

"Then nothing else matters…except of course the fact that I think you caught yourself a fish."

Joel felt the tug on his line. He'd thought he felt it a moment ago, but he was too busy with his thoughts to notice.

"What do I do?" Joel asked as the fish pulled away from him, still attached to the line.

"First off, don't panic and let's ease that big fella in. You've got this."

"I sure do," Joel said, feeling as though not only could he master fly-fishing, but with a little help from friends and family, he might be able to master just about everything else in his life, as well.

WHY THE CITY COUNCIL of Briggs, Idaho, ever decided to hold its annual fish fry during the third week of October had always been a wonder to most of the folks who lived in the town, and Callie was no exception. The weather during the third week of October could vary from a balmy sixty degrees to a chilly thirty-five, and the sun could be all but nonexistent.

Fortunately for everyone concerned, the day had turned into a miracle of sorts with a high of sixty-five and a low somewhere in the fifties. The sun had peeked through the clouds early that morning and refused to let those cottony clouds have their way. They floated by and never once did they linger. The tall grasses and trees had turned to their deepest reds, oranges and yellows, warming the entire canyon that seemed reflected in the winding Snake River as it journeyed over rocks and stones to the grand Columbia River and eventually the Pacific Ocean.

It was perhaps the most perfect day on record for the annual fish fry, and at least half the town had gathered along the banks of the Snake River to participate. Of course, there would be no fish fry without the fish, so the first order of business was the Briggs Whopping Fish Tale Contest, caught solely with fly rods. There were contests for adults and for children. Also, there was a contest for the catch-and-release group, so anyone who wanted to participate could try for the coveted prizes.

The biggest fish caught for the day would be honored with a bright blue ribbon, three hundred dollars in gift cards from the local shops and restaurants in Briggs, and a six-inch resin trophy of a lifelike rainbow trout with its mouth gaping. The fish itself was silver in color, with black spots over its entire body, dorsal and caudal fins. A distinctive bright rainbow of colors traveled along each side as it rode on a wave.

Callie's brother, Carson, her dad and her sister Kenzie had all won the coveted first-place trophy over the years. Callie had won two second-place trophies and three third-place trophies, but had yet to win the coveted first place.

She had bet Carson that this would be her year, but secretly she knew she hadn't practiced nearly enough. She'd be lucky if she came in third, which came with a white ribbon, a small silver trophy and fifty dollars' worth of gift cards.

Her second-place silver trophies sat on a shelf in her bedroom, along with the yellow ribbons. Back when she'd won them, there were no gift cards associated with the prize. The gift cards were a recent addition brought about by the forward-thinking mayor, Sally Hickman, who liked to rally the local shopkeepers for a good cause. Getting more townsfolk to participate in the annual fish fry seemed to be one of them.

Most of the Granger family participated, with Dodge Granger and his plucky wife, Edith, casting deeper out in the river from a small boat this year. Milo Gump and his wife, Amanda, who owned Holy Rollers bakery, Spud Drive In and Belly Up Tavern, had staked out their chunk of shoreline along with Sammy Hastings and his family, owners of Sammy's Smokehouse. Hank Marsh and his teenage grandson, Tommy, were there, along with countless other folks who populated the city of Briggs.

Then there were the out-of-town folks who had driven in for the day. The river swarmed with men, women, teens and younger children who all seemed to enjoy participating in the event, along with a few folks who sat along the shore in lawn chairs watching all the fun on this beautiful day.

"So, I'm ready to win this thing," Joel said as he sneaked up on Callie, who stood at the shoreline holding her fly rod in one hand and the line in the other.

Despite any lasting apprehensions, a hot streak of happiness bumped at her heart. She had hoped he'd come today. This more open and honest Joel Darwood was slowly winning her over, and she had no intention of trying to quell her growing feelings for him. Instead, she wanted to see where they would lead her.

"You think so?" she said, turning to him.

He slipped his hand around her waist, and a surge of heat swept through her body. She hadn't seen him since the previous Saturday at the birthday party for Wade's nephew. Polly or Wade had driven Emma to and from school last week, which had been fine with Callie. She'd needed some time to digest all that she'd learned about the lies that Sarah had told, and Joel's reaction to them.

In her mind, the fact that he could admit his reaction back then had been wrong went a long way in building up his new sincere character. Her trust in him was growing stronger and deeper.

Plus there was her ongoing issue with Emma. Wheezy had not fully recovered from his cold, so Callie had quarantined him in his own little cage away from the children, but still close enough to his sibling, Squeezy. Emma had fussed about it all week, and even found a way to take him out of his cage to hold him when Callie had repeatedly told her not to.

Emma simply wouldn't obey her and Callie didn't know what she could do to change that.

"Yep. Practiced all week." He did a few air moves pretending to cast his line out into the water. Callie had to admit, his movements were spot-on.

"Wade been teaching you?"

"He gave me a crash course and I kept going. Practiced every morning for three hours solid."

"Is that why I didn't see you at school with Emma?"

"Exactly. Needed my time alone. Polly thinks I have a good chance. We went fishing yesterday and I caught a monster rainbow trout, cleaned and filleted it, then shoved it in the freezer. Looking forward to catching the biggest one today."

Callie liked his new confidence, but she doubted if he could deliver. Fly-fishing took a lot of time and patience to master.

"You're pretty sure of yourself, aren't you?" They walked out into the river together. Callie and Joel both wore knee-high rubber black boots over water-resistant field pants and jackets under easy-dry pocket vests. Callie figured Wade or Polly must have taken him shopping over the Idaho border to Jackson, Wyoming, at the outfitter store. His now well-worn gray cowboy hat was slung low on his forehead, shading those gorgeous, piercing blue eyes of his from the bright sunshine.

"Actually, I'm here because I get to spend time with you. If I catch a fish or two in the process, I'll consider the day a complete success."

"Flattery will get you everywhere." She chuckled, easily teasing him now that she had decided to let down her guard…at least a little…and try to enjoy the festivities.

"Then my work here is done." And he leaned in to kiss her, but she nudged him back.

"Not until you catch at least one substantial-sized fish or everyone will think you shirked your responsibility. Today is all about the fish fry tonight, and that means we need a lot of fish. So get catching."

"Yes, ma'am," Joel said and walked a few feet away from her, closer to Hank Marsh, to prepare himself for his task.

She watched as a geared-up Joel took time to hold the rod in his right hand, then carefully placed his left foot forward and his right foot a little farther back. He squared his shoulders, pulled some line off the reel and let it drop into the water at his feet. Some perfect false roll-casting followed, so he wouldn't hook anyone behind him, abruptly stopping the momentum of his forearm at twelve and two o'clock. He then allowed the line to slip through his index finger and thumb during the moment, landing the fly way out in the center of the river.

"You sure you've only been at this a week?" she called out after him.

He nodded his head. "Yep. I guess I'm a natural," he said as he demonstrated to Hank how to cast a line out even farther.

"And then some. It's like you've been angling your whole life," Hank Marsh said in a loud voice as he followed Joel's instructions.

"Seems you finally found your niche, Joel Darwood," Callie teased, completely surprised by how well Joel had taken to fly-fishing when for most people, proper casting was next to impossible to master. "You were meant to live in the country."

"That's the plan, Ms. Callaghan Grant."

Their voices carried over the rippling river without much effort.

"You have a plan?" Callie asked, ribbing him, delighted to see him adjusting to the environment, making friends with Hank, slipping into the event as if he'd participated many times before.

"Oh, yeah, and so far, it's working perfectly."

"Don't count your chickens," Hank Marsh told him while focusing on his line drifting in the river.

"Chickens have never been very reliable. I'm more into trusting my gut," Joel countered.

"And what does your gut tell you?" Callie asked, enjoying the banter.

The two men suddenly became excited over a fish on the end of Hank's hook. Hank carefully reeled it in closer as Joel went out to meet it with his net. Once Joel scooped it up, he let out a loud, "Oh, man!"

"What did he catch?" Callie asked as she made her way to the two men.

"The winning Kamloops," Hank Marsh said as more people started wading toward them.

And sure enough, by the end of the day, Hank Marsh, with Joel's help had, in fact, caught the largest fish, a twenty-six-pound Kamloops, a type of rainbow trout that was known to grow big and fast.

THE ACTUAL FISH FRY took place in the town square, where the Red Neck Villains played bluegrass music in the gazebo, kids had their faces painted, Nettie O'Leary sold her raw local honey and Sam Cook sold his homemade habanero-blueberry jelly. Other locals sold everything from kettle corn to organic baby clothes.

The day had been long and enjoyable, with a trophy for Hank Marsh, Amanda Gump and a few other folks from town. It seemed that all Joel did for the better part of the day was introduce himself to everyone he could, which surprised Callie. She knew he'd turned over a new leaf, she just didn't know that leaf happened to be an entire olive branch.

Emma had won a trophy in the kid's category of catch-and-release for the third-biggest rainbow trout. Joel had been beside himself with joy when she'd won and had made a fuss, something his own dad would never have done. According to Joel, his dad had always refrained from public displays of emotion, and for that matter, he refrained from private displays, as well.

"I intend to break that stiff, emotionless pattern of my dad's," Joel had said. "Emma deserves a whole world of public praise for winning a trophy today. That took a lot of work on her part and she needs a ton of credit!"

Then he'd twirled his daughter around and proceeded to praise her for the next half hour. It was actually fun to watch him not only praise her, but tell everyone who was around them that she'd won.

Callie liked his bravado and how much he celebrated Emma's victory. He was fun to be around and Emma was a delight, as well.

All day long, Callie could barely think of anything else but how Joel's lips had felt on hers. She felt certain that distraction had lost her a trophy today. Her biggest catch was a three-pound sturgeon, hardly a contender.

She'd wanted to kiss Joel earlier that day when they'd first met out on the river, then later after Hank pulled in the winning trout, and when Joel began his open praise for Emma. She felt drawn to him even though she wasn't quite sure if he was playing the flame and she the moth.

Now, as night fell on Briggs, while Callie sat across from Joel at one of the long tables set up to accommodate the participants and watched him interact with Emma, who didn't seem to want to agree to anything, who had become prickly and refused to cooperate with her dad, Callie tried her best to ignore the situation and let Joel handle it. Callie reminded herself that she was Emma's teacher, not her mother.

Emma could be playful and loving, and Callie liked being around her during those times, but there were other times when she could be so downright ornery that Callie didn't know if she could ever learn to accept that kind of behavior. The child tested her patience like none other.

"I want a butterfly painted on my cheek, like Mary has on her face, Daddy," Emma told her dad after she'd refused to eat any of the fish. As it turned out, Emma had decided she didn't like fish, nor did she like coleslaw, and she especially disliked baked potatoes. "I don't want this food, Daddy. I don't like it, and I'm not hungry."

"You should at least try it, kitten. If you take a couple mouthfuls of your fish, along with some coleslaw, you can get your face painted. Aunt Polly will take you."

She shook her head and crossed her arms over her chest in defiance.

Callie refused to bite and instead drank down her cola.

"I don't want to," Emma protested, then pushed her dish away, causing it to slip off the table and land upside down on the grass. She looked up at Joel, guilt staining her little face, knowing perfectly well she'd done something very wrong.

"Fine. Say you're sorry, then you can go over to Aunt Polly," Joel told her as he leaned over to pick up her mess.

Emma sat silent for a moment as Joel cleaned up her overturned plate.

"Emma, I'm waiting," he demanded, albeit not in a very commanding voice. It sounded more like a plea.

"Sorry," she whispered as she shot up from the table, then ran off to meet her aunt along with Mary, Frankie and a few of the other kids from class.

Callie continued to sip her cola, really trying to hold her tongue, but not being able to when she leaned over and saw the mess Emma had made. Most of her meal had landed on the bench seat and Joel busied himself trying to clean it up.

"What?" Joel said as he glanced up at Callie. "I can hear your thoughts whirling."

"Am I that obvious?"

"Yep. I can tell you didn't like how that went down."

"It's none of my business."

"Maybe not, but you're chomping at the bit wanting to say something about it."

Callie knocked off the rest of her drink, and slammed down the bottle a little too hard on the wooden table. "That's it? That's her punishment for acting like a complete brat?" Once she let go, Callie could hardly contain herself. Emma had been defiant, disrespectful and wasteful with good food.

"What would you like me to do, Callie? It's been a long day, and she's probably tired."

"So you're blaming her bad behavior on fatigue." Callie stood and cleared her side of the table along with Joel's, then discarded everything in the nearby trash bin, careful to put the bottle in with the other recyclables. She really didn't want to get into this with Joel, at least not here, not now.

"What else can it be?"

"Oh, I don't know…complete disregard for your authority, lack of discipline, zero conviction. A child knows when a parent is serious or not. They're always testing authority, which is natural, but Emma has to learn her own self-discipline or no one will want to be around her, not even her friends."

Callie hadn't meant to take her argument that far, but she simply couldn't sit back anymore. He'd asked, so the floodgates were open. She'd seen how he'd behaved with Emma when she started acting out, and

Callie simply couldn't stay silent any longer. She'd studied enough about child behavior while she was preparing to teach kindergarten to know what worked and what didn't, and so far, Joel wasn't cutting it.

Callie braced herself for an argument while Joel dumped Emma's mess into the trash, then he sat back down at the table, looking defeated.

"You're right," he said after a moment. "I'm not very good at this parenting thing. Polly is after me all the time, but Emma's been through a lot in the last few months, and I can't help but give her a pass on most things. I suppose I'll have to toughen up at some point...just not tonight. Not when we've all had such a great day together."

His words deflated Callie's resolve to drive her point home. He had agreed with her. At least that was a start.

"WE DID HAVE a great day, a really great day," Callie said, then came over to the table and sat beside him. He felt as though they'd managed to get past an argument, a good sign. "I'm sorry if I came off a little rough on this subject. It's just that I see a lot of Sarah in Emma, maybe a bit too much, and I'm scared for her."

He took her hand in his and threaded his fingers around hers. He liked how their hands seemed to fit together as if they were made for this. "Don't be. I'll figure it out...with your help, and Polly's, of course. So far, every time I've reached out to someone in this town, it's worked in my benefit. I'm thinking if I reach out to you for some pointers on the right way to get through to Emma, I'll eventually get this parenting thing down."

She smiled. "I'm not saying I'm an expert. I'm just saying…"

He leaned in and kissed her words away. He couldn't help himself. The more time he spent with her, the more he listened to what she had to say about this town, the people, his daughter, the more he wanted to be part of her life—if she'd let him.

The kiss only lasted a few seconds before she pulled away. "Don't do that."

"What?" he asked, sitting back, teasing her.

"Kiss me like that when I'm trying to make a point."

"But you already made your point, and besides, I like it when you scold me like that. It's cute."

"I wasn't scolding you. And cute has nothing to do with…"

He kissed her again. This time she leaned in and kissed him back before she pulled away again.

"You have to stop doing that," she told him, a sweet little grin turning up those gorgeous lips of hers.

"Doing what?"

"Kissing me."

He leaned in again, but she nudged him back. "What's wrong?"

"We're in a public place."

"And?"

"And…people will talk."

He looked around. Absolutely no one was looking their way. "They're all too busy with their own stuff."

"They won't be if this keeps up."

"I don't intend to stop." He kissed her neck, and

the scent of her skin sent a rush of heat over his body. She slid farther away.

"If you're going to kiss me like that, can we at least go someplace less public?"

He gazed around. The band was still playing, and the fish fry after-party didn't look as if it would be ending any time soon.

"Just point me in the right secluded direction and I'm there."

"Follow me." She stood, still holding his hand. "There's a private little park about five minutes from here. No one will be there because of the fish fry."

He ran his fingers down her cheek, then slipped her hair behind her ear. Her skin and hair felt like silk. Just touching her like this clenched his stomach and ignited his blood.

"Just let me tell Polly to keep an eye on Emma for a few minutes."

"A few minutes?" she teased. "Is that all?"

"How about if I tell her we're going for a walk? That we'll be a while."

Callie shrugged. "That's probably a wise decision, considering…"

He chuckled.

"…considering."

Then he kissed her one more time, just to make sure this was really happening.

## Chapter Eleven

Ten minutes later, Joel followed Callie into a small, secluded park complete with an assortment of deep red and golden blooming plants. A number of trees stood tall, ablaze with fall colors, bright orange pumpkins lined the winding walkway, and several benches were scattered throughout the area, beckoning them to take a seat. The sun was quickly setting and cast a warm glow on the surroundings. He felt as if he'd just walked into a secret garden.

Two old-style street lamps sat at either end of the park, ready to illuminate the area as soon as the sun set.

"Part of this is a skating rink in the winter, but the rest of the time, it's simply a place to sit to enjoy the beauty. It's owned by the Skaits family, but they keep it open to the public most of the time, except for an occasional private party. I went to elementary school with the Skaits brothers who take care of all this now."

"It's beautiful. Why didn't Polly tell me about this place?"

"Because up until about six years ago, it was a mess—weeds everywhere, dead plants, trees, and the benches were all broken."

He took her hand and walked alongside of her as she spoke. Her raven hair lying on her shoulders and down her back reminded him of how silky it had felt. He wanted to run his hands through it again, wanted to hold her in his arms, press her body against his and never let her go.

He stopped walking and turned to her. "There's no one around now."

"I know," she said, then stepped in front of him and kissed him, wrapping her arms around his waist as he pulled her in tight, tangling his fingers in her amazing hair, hoping this time she wouldn't pull away. Wouldn't tell him that this couldn't work. That she needed more time.

Instead she moved in closer, kissed him harder, moving her lips over his, parting his lips with hers. When his tongue brushed against hers, it ignited a fire deep within him, one that he'd thought was all but gone. He reached inside her shirt and cupped her breast as her sexy throaty moan sent desire to his very core.

"I think we need to make this a bit more private," he whispered.

She took his hand and led him behind a cluster of trees and vines.

"Private enough?" she asked, brushing her lips over his.

"It'll do, but are you sure about this?" he asked as darkness encircled them, and the two streetlights slowly began to glow, her lovely face illuminated by the amber light.

"Yes," she told him, her voice a faint whisper. "But it doesn't mean I'm in love with you."

"I wouldn't expect that," he told her as he slipped off his light jacket, spread it on the grass and eased her down onto it.

"It just means that we've gotten beyond a lot of our past."

He unbuttoned her blouse and unsnapped her pink lacy bra that easily opened in the front. She drew in a quick breath, then slowly let it out as he ran a thumb over a pink cherry-blossom nipple.

"I like how that sounds."

"That we've gotten beyond a lot of our past?"

"Yes, and how you breathe when I touch you."

"It's a natural reaction," she said as he leaned over and sucked the very tip of her breast while he caressed the other, careful not to chafe her soft skin with his rough, dry hands.

"I'll try to be careful," he told her before he moved his mouth over to her other breast, to her other cherry bud.

"Um, I'm loving your touch," she muttered. "It's a man's touch."

Then she took one of his hands and tenderly kissed the bruises on his knuckles and the rough spots on his palms. He watched as she kissed each finger, then placed his hand back on her breast.

As soon as he touched her, she did it again, that guttural quick intake of air, almost sounding as if he'd surprised her, as if she hadn't been expecting the sensation. The thought heightened his desire for her and brought a flood of their lovemaking memories rushing back. All those days and nights they'd spent together wrapped in passion.

Somehow, he'd never felt like this before, never felt the myriad of emotions that now ran through him.

He knew her body, just as she knew his, but for some reason this time seemed like the first time. Like they were both new to this moment, and the anticipation of it bore deep into him.

He slid his hands down her taut stomach and began to unfasten her jeans. She reached up, slid her hands under his T-shirt and helped slip it over his head. She slowly ran her fingertips over his chest, then over his shoulders and down his arms.

"I love the way you feel, the way you look," she told him in a low, teasing voice, as he pulled her jeans and panties down her legs, stopping at her boots.

"I can't go any further," he told her, as his gaze slowly made its way up her now-naked body. She was truly beautiful, and even more beautiful than he remembered her to be.

"Let me help," she said, and reached up to undo his jeans.

Within their next few breaths, most of their clothing lay on the grass next to them, and he couldn't take his eyes off her gorgeous naked body. He ripped open the condom packet that he'd pulled from his back pocket, then carefully rolled it over his erection.

"Now," she whispered, her legs parting, ready to take him inside her.

But he wanted more, wanted to make this moment last a bit longer.

"I want to taste you first," he said.

She gave him a wicked little smile, sucked in a breath and slid her fingers into his hair as he kissed a trail to her center. She relaxed and gave in to his touch, abandoning any apprehensions she may have had. It didn't take long for her body to quiver from his mouth on her, and when he knew she was close to the edge, he stopped, wanting to fall over that edge with her.

"Joel, please," she said.

"Now," he told her as he slowly glided himself inside her, taking his time at first, feeling her warmth surround him.

"Now," she whispered as she moved her hips to accommodate him.

He moved faster as he stared down at her and she up at him. Their eyes steadfast on each other, their pace increasing until they both fell over the edge in waves of blissful release. So much so that he felt the earth rumble…or was that his phone vibrating in the jacket pocket, which lay under both of them, on the grass?

He rolled off of her then, pulling her in close, ignoring the phone call, telling himself whoever it was would leave a message.

"Is that your phone?" Callie asked as she pushed in closer to him.

Everything that was in him wanted to disregard the vibrating phone, but when the buzz seemed louder than a train whistle and the phone poked him in the ribs, he couldn't ignore it anymore.

"I'm sorry," Joel finally said after the phone began its second bout of vibrations. "I need to take this. It might be Polly."

"Sure," Callie said as she slipped out from under his touch. "I understand."

Joel found his phone, gazed at the screen, then

sat up and tugged on his underwear and jeans. "It's Emma."

"Of course it is," Callie said under her breath, but Joel caught it.

"What's that mean?"

"Nothing. I just meant that...nothing."

Joel stood and answered the call, turning away from Callie.

CALLIE PULLED UP her panties and jeans, fastened her bra and buttoned her shirt. She knew Emma's needs came first, but in this situation, her timing couldn't have been worse.

She had to face the fact that Emma would always have to come first, which was completely understandable, but could she deal with that reality?

She felt like the evil stepmother who was trying to separate a father from his daughter. It was an odd emotion that Callie struggled with. She loved children, loved being around them, loved teaching them, playing with them, and longed to be a mom.

But Emma was different.

There was something about Emma that Callie simply couldn't accept, and it hindered her relationship with Joel. Even now when she'd forgiven Joel for their past and longed for his touch, she didn't know if she could give Emma the love she deserved. And truth be told, she knew it was a package deal.

"Sure, baby, I understand," Joel said into his phone. "I know. I know. Don't cry. I'll be there soon. Put Auntie Polly on the phone, kitten." When he turned back to her she was fully dressed again, staring up at a gorgeous sky filled with stars. The night had finally cooled down and she felt a chill, rubbing her arms for warmth.

"Emma got sick all over herself and wants to go home," he told Callie. "I should've known something was up when she didn't want to eat." He turned back to the phone and made uh-huh sounds. Then he said, "I'll be right there," and disconnected.

He swung around to Callie, who stood next to him now and scooped her up in his arms. Holding her tight against his bare chest. His strong arms encircling her, ratcheting up her desire for him once again. She rested her head on his shoulder for a moment, struggling with a torrent of conflicting emotions.

"You're so cold." He held her closer, rubbing her back for warmth. "Come home with me. Spend the night. Once I get Emma settled, she'll sleep until morning. Then tomorrow we can spend the day together, just the three of us."

Despite how good she felt in his arms, she moved away. "I don't think that's a good idea. Emma's not feeling well, and having me around will only make matters worse."

He slipped his T-shirt over his head, then stepped into his boots, picked up his jacket, gave it a shake and dropped it around Callie's shoulders. "Don't be ridiculous. Emma loves you. She'd be thrilled to spend an entire day with her Miss Callie."

"That's the problem, Joel… Emma." Callie screwed up her courage. Maybe this wasn't the right time, but she had to tell him before…before her feelings for him spiraled out of control. "No matter how I try, I can't seem to warm up to her. There's just something between us that doesn't click. I don't know what it is. If I did, I could fix it."

Joel walked in closer to Callie. "That can't be true. I've seen you two together. I can tell you love her. You're kind, and you take the time to explain things to her. She does well with that. She's learning limits."

"Yes, I'm kind to her. I explain things to her, but do I love her? Can I love her? I don't know. I don't know if I could ever love her. She's hard to control, Joel. She purposely takes the toys her classmates are playing with and won't give them back. She'll swipe their crayons and break them on purpose. And Wheezy, I've told her time and again to leave him alone while he's recovering, but she won't listen. Whenever I'm not looking she pulls him out of his pen and tries to get him to hop over whatever hurdle she's managed to put together. She's a difficult child, Joel."

"Why haven't you told me this before…before I fell in love with you?"

His words stung. She knew that deep inside she'd never stopped loving him, and now more than ever she wanted his love in return, but until she could work out her feelings about Emma, she didn't know how they could ever be together.

"I'm sorry," she said, moving away from him. "I should have told you, but I thought you knew, that you could sense it."

A deep sadness gripped her by the throat as she tried to control the emotion that welled up in her eyes.

Joel ran a hand through his thick hair. Confusion furrowed his forehead. "I love you, Callie, but that little girl has been through way too much. I'm not willing to bring anyone into my life who can't love her as much as I do. I made a promise to myself when Sarah died to be the father Emma deserves, and nothing and no one is going to jeopardize that, not even you...especially not you. I thought it would be different this time, Callie. I've finally grown up and changed. I thought you did, too. I thought you could easily love Emma as your own, if not for me, then for Sarah. You said you once loved Sarah like a sister. This isn't how you would love one of your sister's children, Callie. There wouldn't be a barrier of intolerance. Love would come automatically." His phone rang, and he glanced down at the screen. "It's Emma. I have to go."

Then he turned and walked away, leaving Callie alone to face the cold hard fact that Sarah had not only played a game with his emotions, but she'd hit the jackpot with his love for Emma. In Sarah's own mixed-up and tragic way, she had managed to turn Joel into a committed dad, and a true cowboy whom Callie admired and loved more than she ever thought possible.

IF JOEL THOUGHT he was going to get any sleep on that Saturday night after everything that had happened with Callie, he was badly mistaken. Not only couldn't he sleep, but he'd been wrong about Emma sleeping through the night. She kept waking up with bad dreams, crying for her mommy.

It broke his heart.

"It's okay, kitten. I'm here," Joel had cooed as he knelt next to Emma's bed and ran his hand over her damp forehead, pushing her hair back from her face.

"But I want my mommy. Where's my mommy? Can we go home now, so mommy can find us? I think she doesn't know where we are. That's why she's not here."

Joel hated to see his daughter in so much pain, her little face contorted with sadness, her eyes wet with tears as she clung to Joel.

"We've talked about this, baby. Your mommy's not lost. She's in heaven."

"I don't want her to be in heaven. I want her here, with us."

"I know, but she can't be, at least not physically. But I guarantee that she's watching over us."

"But I can't see her, Daddy. I can't feel her kisses. I don't like heaven. It's a terrible place. Do they keep her in a cage like where Miss Callie keeps Wheezy? Is that why she can't come see us? Is she in a cage?"

"No, baby. Heaven is a beautiful place with trees and flowers and all the things that your mommy loves. She's free to walk around or fly if she wants to."

"Is that why she doesn't come back, because she likes heaven better than she likes it here with us? Because she doesn't like me anymore?"

Her questions tore at his heart. "Your mommy loves you, kitten. She will always love you, no matter what. Just like I will always love you. And Aunt Polly loves you."

"Miss Callie doesn't love me. She was mad at me tonight, Daddy. I didn't mean for my plate to fall off the table. I didn't mean to push it that hard, honest."

"When someone gets angry with something you do, that doesn't mean they don't love you. It just means that for the moment, they're upset with your actions. That's all. Miss Callie loves you, kitten," Joel told

Emma, knowing perfectly well how Callie felt about her. "We all do."

"I don't think so, Daddy. I do mean things in school sometimes, and Miss Callie gets real mad. I don't like it when she gets mad at me, but sometimes I can't stop myself from being bad."

Joel could identify with that kind of behavior. He'd participated in it for most of his life. "You know what helps me from doing mean things?"

"What?"

"I think about you, and how much I love you, and how much you love me. Then just like that, all the mean goes away. All that's left is love. Maybe you should try it when mean comes knocking on your door. Think about how much I love you, and how much your mommy loves you, and Auntie Polly."

She sat up and spread out her little arms, a big smile brightened up her sweet face. "And how much I love everyone."

Joel spread his arms, as well. "Everyone!"

Then he gave his child a big tight hug, tucked her under the covers and kissed both her cheeks, her forehead and her nose.

She giggled. "That tickles, Daddy."

"Get some sleep, kitten. I'm right up the hall if you need me."

"Can you play my ballerina music box first, please, Daddy?"

"Absolutely," Joel said, then cranked the little silver button on the back of the music box her mom had given her when she turned three. She always kept it on her nightstand and it played every night at bedtime.

As Joel left the room, the tinkling music echoing

in his ears, he knew he'd made the right decision with Callie; no matter how much it ripped his heart apart, his Emma came first.

CALLIE HAD SPENT the night in a state of perpetual unrest, something she'd been wrestling with a lot lately. Not only hadn't she been able to sleep, but when she finally emerged from her bedroom in search of coffee, sometime after ten in the morning, she ran into her brother, Carson, who had stopped by with a pink box filled with scones, muffins and pastries from Holy Rollers. He'd always had a knack for turning up when she needed him most. It was uncanny.

"What's the occasion?" Callie asked, barely able to think from lack of sleep. She knew she had to be a hot mess, but she also knew her brother had seen her looking much worse. She wore her warmest long red robe over dark blue sweats, her hair was up in some sort of ponytail, and she hadn't bothered removing her makeup before she went to bed. Plus, she'd cried for most of the night, so she knew her nose was beet red and her eyes had to be puffy and bloodshot.

"I thought that you might need a little cheering up this morning. I bought your favorite dark cherry muffin and a large caramel latte, a drink Amanda Gump said was your favorite."

He held up the beautiful, extra-large white paper cup, and Callie near about cried.

"God bless Amanda!"

Callie took a quick sip, sighed, sat down at the kitchen table and opened the box of goodies. Carson pulled out the chair across from her and made himself comfortable at the long rectangular table.

"Whenever you're ready," he said, taking a long drink from his own white paper cup.

"I don't want to talk about it," Callie told her brother in no uncertain terms.

She went right for the cherry muffin and took a big fat bite. Nothing had ever tasted so good in her entire life...or maybe just in the last couple weeks, ever since she'd decided to give Joel Darwood another chance.

"You have to. I didn't drive all the way over here just to bring you doughnuts."

"Muffins."

"Whatever. What happened last night between you and Joel?"

She drank her latte, savoring its rich, creamy caramel flavor. Perfect. The staff at Holy Rollers really knew how to make a latte.

"Nothing."

"That's the problem, right there."

She stopped midchew. "What's that supposed to mean?"

"I saw you two sneak off. In fact, half the town saw you, but Joel came back alone, about twenty minutes later. Not enough time for...well...serious stuff to happen. I can't be one hundred percent sure, but I'd bet the ranch nothing...*happened*. And if it did, it couldn't have been very meaningful. Why is that exactly? Except for some strange dudes our family forced you into dating, you haven't been serious about anyone until Joel moved into town. From what I've seen and what I've heard, he's a stand-up kind of guy, great with his daughter, treats Sarah's aunt with respect, has learned how to maintain and run her ranch, and even helped Hank Marsh win a trophy. After all that, for some reason, you and he can't seem to pull it together. Why not? What's the holdup?"

Callie hated when her brother tried to get her to open up before she was ready to confide in him. Sure he was great at seeing the big picture, and maybe she'd been going to him lately for advice, but this morning she wasn't interested in landscapes, not when she could focus in on a tiny flower...a tiny flower like Emma.

"He broke my heart, and I'm terrified he's going to do it again," she told him, hoping the overview would be enough and he would leave her to her coffee and muffin. She intended to consume two muffins this morning, and maybe a couple scones.

"That's part of it, but what else? What's really behind this, Callie? With four sisters, I didn't grow up wearing blinders. I know when one of you has something eating away at her insides. Tell me the real problem."

Callie finished off her cherry muffin and went for a blueberry scone.

Carson pulled the box away.

"Seriously?" She slapped the table.

"Not until you tell me."

"I just did."

He shook his head. "Nope. I'm not buying it."

She stood and reached for the box. He stood and pulled it away.

"This is baked-goods blackmail," she told him.

She reached for the box again, but Carson held it way up over his head. She was desperate now. He knew her comfort food during times of trauma was something sweet, and he was taunting her with it.

This was so unfair.

She relented. "Fine, but you can't hate me if I tell you."

"You're my sister. It would take a lot for me to hate you."

"Oh, so you *could* hate me?"

"Okay, maybe not hate, but if the situation warranted it, we could all dislike each other. But I'd always love you. You're my sister." He smirked.

"Good to know."

"Just tell me what's wrong."

"It's Emma. I can't seem to accept her, to like her."

"Does Joel know this?"

"To a degree, yes. I told him last night."

He let out a long whistle, pushed back his black cowboy hat and placed the pink box of yummy delights on the table, then he sat down, hard. Callie sat, as well, but didn't take a scone. Now that she'd admitted it out loud to her brother, her stomach felt queasy.

"That's rich, don't you think?"

"What, because you said you could actually dislike me?"

"Well, yeah, there's that, but also Emma is Sarah's daughter. That little girl looks enough like her mom to be her double. I'm thinking that has a lot to do with your feelings for her."

Callie wrapped her arms across her tummy. She suddenly felt cold, as if all the blood had drained from her body.

"That doesn't mean anything. It's her personality. She's hard to be around. You don't know what that child is like. I ask her to do something and she does the exact opposite, and she can be spiteful to the other children. And don't even get me started on how she gives Joel and Polly sass. She's downright defiant!"

"So was Sarah, at least to everyone but you. As I recall, you loved her rebellious streak. How she wouldn't be deterred by anyone. How she always knew what she wanted, and wasn't afraid to go get it."

"She wanted Joel and she took him from me, her best friend. Now Emma wants Joel. She wants all his time and energy and love. There's nothing left for me."

As soon as she admitted her innermost feelings, she felt as if she'd been hit by a bolt of lightning.

"Do you hear yourself, Callaghan Grant? Do you hear your resentment toward a young child? For Sarah's child?"

The fact that she'd finally articulated feelings that had been swirling around in her for weeks, brought up a well of emotion she'd been doing everything to keep secret, even from herself. And now, a door had opened and she could see what had been hidden behind it, what she'd locked away.

"Oh, Carson. I've been so blind. So filled with my own pity. What's wrong with me? I'm a horrible person. Joel should hate me…you should hate me. Everyone in this family and this town should hate me. Maybe even the world."

"Come here," Carson said. They stood, and he wrapped his strong arms around her as she sobbed on his shoulder. She remembered all the other countless times she'd cried on her big brother's shoulder. All her sisters had. He was always there for them. But would he really be there for her now? Now, when he knew how horrible she'd been acting toward an innocent child?

"Nobody hates you, at least I don't think they do... well, maybe Joel does, but you might still be able to fix that if you're honest with him. If you tell him the truth like you just told me. Of course, getting the truth out of you or any one of our sisters can be like birthing a breech calf. Sometimes I just gotta reach in there and pull it out."

She looked up at him, smiling from his little visual dig. After all, he was still her *annoying* brother.

"Oh, thanks," Callie said. "You just compared me...and our sisters...to a birthing cow. That makes me feel so much better."

She sobbed even louder.

## Chapter Twelve

Callie had spent most of Sunday doing chores around the ranch, not really talking to anyone. She was still coping with the fact that she'd been taking her resentment out on a child when all her adult life, she'd been wanting children of her own. What kind of mother would she make if she couldn't love Emma, who needed all the love and kindness she could give her?

When dinner came around, and her mother entertained her usual houseful of guests, Callie locked herself in her room feigning an oncoming cold. Her mom prepared a plate, but all Callie ate was the homemade apple pie with three scoops of ice cream.

She didn't fall asleep until sometime around four in the morning, and when the alarm went off, she slept right through it. She called Mrs. Pearl in the office at school to tell her she'd be late. Callie felt as if she'd been run over by a bus, a great big double-decker bus. Not only were her emotions fried, but she'd been living on sugar and coffee for two days straight. To say she felt sick was an understatement. She had cultivated a headache that would bring a two-hundred-pound man to his knees.

Just as Callie walked into her classroom, the sound

of the bell ripped through her head causing her headache to intensify…or was the bell actually the piercing scream from one of her students just outside the back door?

Inside, Mrs. Pearl, a normally unflappable woman in her fifties, let out a little yelp and ran out of the room, saying she would get security.

Before Callie could get her bearings, most of the children ran to the back door and crowded the open doorway.

Another wail, then some crying.

"It's Emma, Miss Callie. She must be hurt," Frankie told her, his normally bright face showing agonizing concern for his friend.

"Children, let me through," Callie ordered in a calm voice. She told herself to remain unruffled no matter what, despite the fact that her heart raced and her throat felt as though it was caught in a vise. The children depended on the adult to handle whatever situation came up, irrespective of how bad it might be.

She assumed that Emma must have fallen or hurt herself pretty badly, and from the high pitch of her screams, it might be critical. Callie pulled her phone out of her pocket as she neared the door, in case she had to call 9-1-1 and Joel.

Her students stepped aside as Callie approached. Emma's sobbing and screeching wasn't letting up, Adrenaline heightened Callie's apprehensions. She prayed for this emergency, whatever it was, to please end well.

When she finally saw Emma racked with tears, crying and shaking while standing in front of the bunny hutch, Callie knew something tragic must have happened to one of the rabbit, and not to Emma. Some of Callie's dire fears faded as she slipped her phone back into her pocket and coolly approached Emma, thoroughly relieved that nothing bad had happened to her. In that moment, once all the barriers had been stripped away, and all the misplaced resentment vanished, Callie realized how much she truly cared about Emma, only she hadn't wanted to admit it even to herself. She'd been so busy trying to safeguard her heart that she'd almost pushed away the one child who needed her most... Sarah's child.

She turned back to her students, who were huddled in the open doorway like frightened puppies. "Children, please go back inside and take a seat on the rug. I'll be there in one minute."

None of them budged as Emma's distress escalated with another ear-piercing shriek when she spotted Callie walking toward her. This time she didn't take another breath until her lips began to turn blue.

Callie immediately went over, knelt on one knee and folded Emma into her arms. At first Emma sought out the warmth, but then without warning, Emma took in a breath, screamed again and fought Callie's embrace. She squirmed, pushed and scratched, trying her best to release herself from Callie's grasp.

"No! No! I don't...want...you. Something...bad happened. I want my daddy."

Callie brushed the sweat away from Emma's forehead and tried to soothe her. Seeing her this upset tore at Callie's heart. "Emma. Emma, look at me, sweetheart. I can't help you if you don't calm down. I need to know what's wrong. Take a breath and talk to me."

But Emma wanted no part of it. Instead, she struggled and wriggled out of Callie's grasp. Callie held on to one of her arms as Emma pulled back with all her might. Callie was afraid if she let go, Emma would fall backward on the concrete and hit her head or hurt her back. Callie tried to get a better hold on her. Emma refused to give in.

Frankie ran over to them. "It's okay, Emma. It's okay. Don't cry. Holy moly, Emma, what's wrong? Did you fall?"

Emma shook her head, relaxing for a moment, which gave Callie the opportunity to get a better hold. "It's…Wheezy. What's…wrong with Wheezy?"

Frankie peeked into the hutch and poked at something. He sniffled, then said, "He's dead. Wheezy's dead."

Then Frankie began to wail, as well.

Emma shrieked again, her little body stiff with despair. The other children had apparently heard Frankie and began to cry, some of them sobbing and yelling out Wheezy's name. Soon, the children surrounded Callie, all wailing with abandon.

Emma stopped pulling, so Callie let her go in order to check on Wheezy, and sure enough, poor little Wheezy lay on his side, stiff as a board, while Squeezy sat huddled in the corner of his own hutch, his breathing labored and fast.

Callie slipped off her sweater, wrapped it around Wheezy and removed the beloved creature from his little cage.

As soon as Emma realized what was happening, she wept louder and ran off into the school yard, with all the other children following close behind in a single line, like distraught ducklings following their mama. Other students and their teachers were now pouring out of their classrooms to add to the commotion.

John Keswick, the twentysomething first-grade teacher, seemed to understand the situation almost immediately. He carefully took Wheezy from Callie and laid him on top of the hutch, high enough away from the children's eyes. "Let's just put him up here for the time being," he said to Callie, "where he'll be out of the way, until you decide what to do with him."

"Thanks," Callie told him, grateful that he had a temporary solution. It gave her a little respite from the situation, enabling her mind to reset itself out of the chaos.

"And it's only Monday," John said with a sly grin. Then he corralled his students and somehow managed to get them all back inside the school.

The second-grade class, under Mr. Zeke Crawly's strict tutelage, wasn't so eager to listen and instead wanted to see a dead rabbit. Some of them already had their phones out eager to capture Wheezy's lifeless body in digital form with the intention of sending the wretched images into cyberspace.

Callie stood her ground and wouldn't let any of them near Wheezy.

"I always thought your petting zoo was a bad idea," Mr. Crawly said with a haughty tone to his strident voice. "And that child needs to be disciplined with a firm hand, which her father obviously doesn't have the stomach for. She's disrupted your entire class. Nothing worse than a pushover parent with an out-of-control child."

The man riled Callie to her core. "For one thing,

'that child' just lost an animal she adored. She's merely reacting to that terrible loss. You have no idea what she's been through in the last few months, so back off. She's one brave little girl who knows what she wants and isn't afraid to stand up for herself. And, for your information, her father is the finest dad I've ever met. He's kind, loving, attentive and understanding of a child's needs, which is more than I can say for you as a teacher."

His students cheered. And in that instant, Callie knew she would be in trouble with the school board for what she'd just said. Funny thing was, she didn't care. It was about time someone stood up to him, and it was about time she stood up for Emma and Joel.

"You'll regret this," he whispered.

"No," she said, "you will."

Then she ran out into the school yard to retrieve her peeps, who were now huddled around Emma.

WHEN JOEL HAD received the call from Mrs. Pearl that Emma was causing a disruption in her class at school and he needed to pick her up, the lump in his throat seemed about as big as a bowling ball.

He knew that whatever Emma had done now, and with the way Callie felt about his daughter, that once again, she would probably be expelled. He ran different scenarios over in his head as he raced to school. Finding another school for her would be a challenge, especially since the nearest one was over forty-five minutes away in a different county.

He could homeschool her, or at least maybe Polly could, or maybe he could hire someone to come in and teach Emma.

But he couldn't get around the fact that all Emma's friends were at this school. She loved her new friends, and the bunnies, the turtles and the fish in Callie's classroom. He didn't have the heart to tell her she couldn't see them anymore.

He wondered if he could somehow change Callie's mind, at least about school. Unfortunately, from the way she had spoken about Emma, he knew that might be impossible. Besides, he owed it to his daughter to find a teacher who genuinely liked her.

Once again, Joel thought that trying to put down roots might not be something he and his daughter were cut out for. Every time they tried, something went wrong.

Thing was, this town had grown on him, had grown on Emma. He liked who he'd become from living here, from meeting the townsfolk and from being with Callie. Besides, both he and Emma depended on Polly, and she depended on them. No way could he start over somewhere else without her.

He pulled his SUV into a parking space, turned off the ignition, jumped out and took off for the front steps without bothering to lock up his rig. He had to find a way to make this work, despite what anyone said to him this morning, despite what Callie had said to him the other night.

As he walked to the office he thought for sure he'd see Emma sitting on a bench, waiting for her father, like she had in the last three schools she'd been expelled from. When he arrived at the office and didn't see her, he peeked inside, but didn't see her there, either.

On a hunch, he left and walked down the quiet hallway, passing walls decorated with artwork that the children had done, Emma's picture of a horse family standing next to a barn was still on display. There was a massive bulletin board announcing various events for Halloween, including the play Emma would be in, parent-teacher night and a bake sale that Polly and Emma were already planning for.

It was up to him to make the case for his daughter. Up to him to find a way to convince Callie and whoever else he needed to talk to that Emma needed this…that he needed this.

When he came up on Callie's classroom, the door was open, and the only two people inside were Emma and Callie. Emma sat on Callie's lap, resting her head on Callie's shoulder, legs slung over Callie's, listening intently to every word Callie said. They sat in the middle of the round rug on the floor. Joel spotted the rest of Callie's class out in the school yard through the open doorway. Mrs. Pearl was with them. Neither Callie nor Emma had seen him when he approached, and he quietly moved just behind the wall and listened.

"Your mama loved to ride a horse. Aunt Polly taught her when she was your age. The summers your mama came to visit were some of the best times I ever had. I loved your mama like a sister, just like I love you."

"Like a sister?"

"Not exactly. I love you like your mama's daughter… like my own daughter."

Raw emotion welled up inside of Joel. He could hear the love in Callie's voice, in her words. He didn't know what had caused the change in her feelings for Emma, but he was thankful that it had.

"Your mama and I did everything together," Callie said. "There was one summer when our team even won the spud tug at the county fair."

"What's a spud tug?" Emma asked, carefully repeating the words.

"It's where two groups of kids or adults hold on to opposite sides of a rope and pull. The thing is, they have to do it over a big pit of sticky, gooey, cold mashed potatoes. The losing side usually falls in."

Emma giggled. "I want to do that."

"Fall into the gooey mashed potato pit?"

Joel grinned. He knew what his daughter would say next.

"Uh-huh. Mashed potatoes are my favorite." Then she giggled again.

All the tension that Joel had been carrying around since he'd received the phone call drained out of him, like water through an open faucet. His shoulders relaxed and his fists opened.

"We'll see what we can do about that next year," Callie told her, a lilt to her voice.

"Did my mama ever talk about me?"

"Well, she didn't know you back then. It was before you were born. But she and I would talk about all the children we were going to have. And you know what? Your mama always said she was going to have a girl first, a baby girl she would name Emma. And here you are."

"She knew I would be her daughter?"

Joel could hear the excitement in Emma's voice as he leaned against the wall, happy that Callie was taking the time to share some of her memories of Sarah with Emma. It felt magical and right.

"Yep. She planned for it. She even knew what color eyes you would have."

"Blue!" Emma shouted.

This was news to Joel. He hadn't had many conversations about Emma with Sarah, although she'd never wavered on Emma's name.

"Yes, and blond hair. She knew you would be smart and funny and love animals just like she did. Your mama loved, loved, loved animals of all kinds."

"I love, love, love animals, just like my mama."

He could tell that Callie's words acted like a balm on Emma's longing for Sarah.

"Did my mama love bunnies?"

"Most of all."

"Do you think she can find Wheezy up in heaven?"

"When you say your prayers tonight, if you tell your mama all about Wheezy, I'm sure she'll know exactly what he looks like and be able to find him."

"I don't want to wait until tonight. Can I say my prayers right now?"

"We can say them together. How would that be?"

Joel couldn't hold back the emotion that had built up inside him. Without giving it another thought, he walked into the room. "Can I join you in those prayers?"

"Daddy!" Emma squealed and ran to greet him.

He gathered her up into his arms, twirling her around and giving her the tightest hug ever. Callie stood as he walked over to her. He could see the tears welling up, which only made his love for her grow more deeply.

"Wheezy died, Daddy," Emma said as she stroked his cheek. He turned his focus on Emma as she gazed into his now-tearful eyes. "Don't cry, Daddy. It's okay. He was sick and Miss Callie said it was his time to go to heaven. Just like it was Mama's time. Miss Callie says that Mama loved bunnies the best, like I do. She'll love Wheezy, Daddy. He'll keep her company up in heaven, like he kept me company. All we have to do is tell Mama all about Wheezy and she'll find him. I want Mama to find him real soon, Daddy. Maybe if we all tell her about Wheezy, she'll find him right now, and then Mama won't be lonely anymore."

"I think that's a great idea, baby."

He put Emma down, took Callie's hand and gently brushed his lips against hers.

"Thank you," he whispered. "Thank you for loving my daughter."

"Seems I always did," Callie told him. "Once I shed the barriers, all that was left was love for you and for Emma."

They gently kissed again, her lips warm on his, his hand holding on to hers, while Emma tugged on his other hand.

"Oh, Daddy. You're kissing Miss Callie."

Joel moved away from Callie and glanced down at his sweet daughter. "Yes, I am, kitten. I hope that's okay with you."

Emma looked up at her dad, then at Callie, then back to her dad. All at once a big smile creased her sweet lips, and Joel knew everything was going to be just fine from now on. "I think it's superfantabulous! I love Miss Callie, Daddy. She's my favorite."

"Mine, too," Joel said, staring into Callie's eyes. "I love Miss Callie with all my heart."

"All my heart," Callie repeated.

"Mine, too!" Emma said. "And I bet Mama does, too. Can we tell Mama about Wheezy now?"

"We sure can, kitten."

"Miss Callie, do you think they have bunny hopping contests in heaven?"

"I'm sure they do," Callie told her, grinning.

"Oh that's good, then Wheezy will be happy, too. He loves to hop, hop, hop over everything!"

"He sure does, kitten."

Then as they sat in a circle on the rug, and bowed their heads to tell Sarah about Wheezy, Joel knew in his heart that for once in his life, not only had he found true love, but he'd found a home.

# *Epilogue*

The crowd inside the covered arena clapped and cheered as Callie walked Squeezy, the Holland lop-eared bunny, out into the colorful competition area. A large square of imitation grass held several hurdles lined up in two neat rows. Looking at them now, they seemed as tall as buildings compared to the hurdles Squeezy had been practicing with inside her classroom for almost six months.

Doubt began to creep into Callie's thoughts as she quickly recounted the previous competitors, two of which had nearly perfect scores.

Tamping down her fears, she gently placed Squeezy on the grass and held tight to his leash. Gazing back at her entire kindergarten class, along with most of their parents, she couldn't help but pull from their enthusiasm and make it her own.

"You can do it, Squeezy!" came a yell from little Mary.

"Go, Squeezy!" Frankie hollered.

"Yay, Squeezy!" someone shouted.

Callie glanced over at Joel, who gave her a thumbs-up and a wide grin, both of which reminded her to breathe. She immediately let out the breath she'd been holding, rolled her shoulders and shook out her hands. She'd been gripping the black leash coming off the H-style harness that wrapped around Squeezy's mid-section with so much force that her hand was beginning to go numb.

"We can do this," she told herself and Squeezy, just in case he was paying attention. "This is nothing you haven't been doing in class for the past six months. Nothing new here. We've got this."

More cheers from everyone that surrounded the white picket fence encircling the compact competition area. In the last few years, the bunny hop had become one of the main attractions at the festival, and this year they had to add a row of bleachers to accommodate everyone. Even her family was there, along with Polly, Wade and the majority of the townsfolk.

Which only heightened Callie's stress level.

Nellie Bent—a girl Callie would forevermore be beholden to, who was the new Miss Russet, thank you very much, and honorary queen of this year's Hearts, Hops and Chocolate festival—called out the countdown.

"On your mark, get set, hop!"

Callie could hardly contain the ball of fluff from doing his thing. He cleared the first vertical jump with room to spare, then he made a dash for the second hurdle, the third and fourth without so much as a hesitation, clearing each one with the grace of a... well...bunny.

A walk over the bunny-sized bridge was next and Callie knew he never really liked this part. He paused for a moment, as if the little darling was building up his courage.

Callie could hear Emma's voice above the din. "C'mon, Squeezy, you're the best!"

Without further hesitation, as if responding to Emma's voice, the little guy took the bridge in a couple bounds, jumped over the next two hurdles, rounded the corner and jumped on the teeter-totter with all the confidence of a gold medalist. Callie had a hard time keeping up with him as he hopped just past the center, causing the bright blue plank to tilt and hit the ground. Then with three powerful hops he jumped off the plank and leaped over the final hurdle, where he waited for his much-deserved applause.

"We did it!" Callie yelled, swooped up Squeezy and hurried toward her class and into Joel's arms. Never in her life had she wanted to win something more than at that moment.

"You two were amazing," Joel told her as he held her tight. "But I never doubted you guys for a minute."

"Holy moly, Miss Callie! Holy moly!" Frankie said, in his deepest voice. "I was so scared I wanted to throw up."

"Me, too," Emma agreed. "But I didn't. I knew Squeezy could do it. I just knew it!"

Callie handed Squeezy to Emma, who had become an expert at handling the bunny. She placed him on her left arm, with his head tucked into her side, with his butt resting in her hand so he wouldn't get frightened. "Can you put Squeezy in his cage, Emma? He must be tired from all the excitement."

"I'll help," Frankie said. Then they worked together carefully to get Squeezy into his cage safe and sound.

Within what seemed like mere seconds, Nellie Bent

announced this year's winners, and Squeezy had, in fact, taken first place.

"You know," Joel said to Callie, "this means that Squeezy has to be a part of our wedding."

"Emma and I wouldn't have it any other way," she teased, smiling.

"Then you accept?"

She chuckled, thinking he couldn't actually be asking her to marry him…in the middle of all this bunny madness. "Was that an actual proposal?"

"Yes, and I can't think of a better time or place to ask you."

"Now? With all of this going on?"

"Exactly, with all of this going on…it's who we are, who I've always wanted to be…with you and Emma."

Then he pulled a small blue box out of his pocket, opened it and held it out for Callie. Her breath caught in her throat when she saw a sparkling pink stone nestled in the center of a silver rose.

He knelt on one knee, and as soon as he did, all her kindergarten peeps must have spotted him, because the little guys swarmed them, giggling.

"Callaghan Grant, I love you with all my heart. Will you marry me?"

Callie could hear her own breathing. No one spoke or laughed. Everyone who had been watching the bunny hop from the stands was now waiting for Callie's response.

"I, um…" But her voice caught in her throat.

"You gotta answer him, Miss Callie, or I'm going to throw up," Frankie said.

"Me, too," Emma chimed in.

Clearing her tight throat, Callie quickly shouted, "Yes! For heaven's sake, yes!"

A collective whoop of joy went up that was so loud Callie was sure she saw Squeezy dance around in his cage.

"Whoo-hoo!" Joel yelled and scooped her up, held her tight and twirled her around. Then he kissed her.

It was during that passionate kiss that she once again realized how everything she'd ever wanted was right there in her arms.

\* \* \* \* \*

*Don't miss the next compelling Briggs, Idaho, romance from* USA TODAY *bestselling author Mary Leo and Harlequin Western Romance, coming in spring 2017!*

# REQUEST YOUR FREE BOOKS!
## 2 FREE NOVELS PLUS 2 FREE GIFTS!

**✦ HARLEQUIN®**

# ♥Western ♥Romance

## ROMANCE THE ALL-AMERICAN WAY!

**YES!** Please send me 2 FREE Harlequin® Western Romance novels and my 2 FREE gifts (gifts are worth about $10). After receiving them, if I don't wish to receive any more books, I can return the shipping statement marked "cancel." If I don't cancel, I will receive 4 brand-new novels every month and be billed just $4.74 per book in the U.S. or $5.49 per book in Canada. That's a savings of at least 12% off the cover price! It's quite a bargain! Shipping and handling is just 50¢ per book in the U.S. and 75¢ per book in Canada.* I understand that accepting the 2 free books and gifts places me under no obligation to buy anything. I can always return a shipment and cancel at any time. Even if I never buy another book, the two free books and gifts are mine to keep forever.

154/354 HDN GJ5V

| | |
|---|---|
| Name | (PLEASE PRINT) |

| | |
|---|---|
| Address | Apt. # |

| | | |
|---|---|---|
| City | State/Prov. | Zip/Postal Code |

Signature (if under 18, a parent or guardian must sign)

### Mail to the **Reader Service:**
**IN U.S.A.:** P.O. Box 1867, Buffalo, NY 14240-1867
**IN CANADA:** P.O. Box 609, Fort Erie, Ontario L2A 5X3

**Want to try two free books from another line?**
**Call 1-800-873-8635 or visit www.ReaderService.com.**

* Terms and prices subject to change without notice. Prices do not include applicable taxes. Sales tax applicable in N.Y. Canadian residents will be charged applicable taxes. Offer not valid in Quebec. This offer is limited to one order per household. Not valid for current subscribers to Harlequin Western Romance books. All orders subject to credit approval. Credit or debit balances in a customer's account(s) may be offset by any other outstanding balance owed by or to the customer. Please allow 4 to 6 weeks for delivery. Offer available while quantities last.

**Your Privacy**—The Reader Service is committed to protecting your privacy. Our Privacy Policy is available online at www.ReaderService.com or upon request from the Reader Service.

We make a portion of our mailing list available to reputable third parties that offer products we believe may interest you. If you prefer that we not exchange your name with third parties, or if you wish to clarify or modify your communication preferences, please visit us at www.ReaderService.com/consumerchoice or write to us at Reader Service Preference Service, P.O. Box 9062, Buffalo, NY 14240-9062. Include your complete name and address.

HWR16

SPECIAL EXCERPT FROM

# ⬦HARLEQUIN®

# *Western Romance*

*Archer Boone's work is his life. When the funding
for his horse refuge is in jeopardy, he needs to focus.
So why is he distracted by Eden Monroe and her
two adorable daughters?*

*Read on for a sneak preview of
A COWBOY TO CALL DADDY by Sasha Summers,
the next book in* **THE BOONES OF TEXAS** *series,
available March 2017 wherever
Harlequin Western Romance books and ebooks are sold.*

"Miss Caraway, I'd like you to work with Fester."

"I have no experience with horses, Dr. Boone."

"Archer." He sat in the chair opposite her. "I know
you've never worked with animals before. But you're
smart. Your eyes…" He cleared his throat before trying
again. "You're smart. Fester seems to respond favorably
to you, and I can show you a few things that might help."

*What about her eyes?* "You can't work with Fester
yourself?"

"He barely tolerates me. I'd like you to help him."

She drew in an unsteady breath. "I can't. Thank you."

"Can't isn't a philosophy I subscribe to, Miss Caraway."

She bit back a smile. She appreciated his determination.
But he wouldn't feel the same when she was a Monroe
again. "Dr. Boone, I'm afraid things might get a bit more
complicated."

He frowned. "Why?"

*Because I'm lying to you about who I am.* "My children are arriving today."

"Children?" His surprise was obvious.

She nodded. "I have two."

He opened his mouth, closed it, then said, "Surely your husband—"

"My personal life is my own, Dr. Boone." She straightened in her chair. "I informed you only so you'd understand my answer to your offer."

He continued frowning at her.

He could frown all he wanted but she wasn't here to help him. She was here for her father.

"I apologize for prying." Archer's expression had faded into something softer, something vulnerable and searching.

"No apologies necessary."

Eden stared—she couldn't help it. He wanted to help Fester, wanted the *animal* to be happy. Yes, he was a little rough around the edges, but he was direct—not rude necessarily. And he was incredibly handsome. So far everything she'd learned about Dr. Boone was good. It would be easier if he'd been misspending grant funds or his work ethic was suspect or his facility was dangerous or out of compliance. None of which was the case. Worse, she found herself respecting his single-minded, detail-oriented, fiery loyalty to his work.

If he ever used that undivided focus on a woman…

*Don't miss A COWBOY TO CALL DADDY*
*by Sasha Summers, available March 2017 wherever*
*Harlequin® Western Romance*
*books and ebooks are sold.*

www.Harlequin.com

## Join for FREE today at
## www.HarlequinMyRewards.com

Earn **FREE BOOKS** of your choice.

Experience **EXCLUSIVE OFFERS** and contests.

Enjoy **BOOK RECOMMENDATIONS**
selected just for you.

**PLUS!** Sign up now
and get **500** points
right away!

MYR16R

# Love the Harlequin book you just read?

Your opinion matters.

Review this book on your favorite
book site, review site, blog or your own
social media properties and share
your opinion with other readers!

**Be sure to connect with us at:**
Harlequin.com/Newsletters
Facebook.com/HarlequinBooks
Twitter.com/HarlequinBooks

# JUST CAN'T GET ENOUGH?

Join our social communities
and talk to us online.

You will have access to the latest
news on upcoming titles and special
promotions, but most importantly,
you can talk to other fans about your
favorite Harlequin reads.

Harlequin.com/Community

Facebook.com/HarlequinBooks

Twitter.com/HarlequinBooks

Pinterest.com/HarlequinBooks